Perseverance Road

Enjoy
Josephine Graven

Josephine (Jo) La Russa Graven

This book is a fictional account of Tom and Flora Cole's lives as they adjusted from having it all to starting over when they had a streak of bad luck. All the characters and events are figments of my imagination. Any resemblance to actual persons, living or dead, business establishments, events or locales are entirely coincidental

www.IntellectPublishing.com

Acknowledgment

I am grateful for those individuals who listened as I shared ideas for this writing, offered suggestions, and questioned realism, clarity and gaps in this story as it evolved. Thank you.

To Mary Ardis, storyteller, writer and illustrator of children's books, who patiently tutored me in writing with clarity. She is my encourager and friend. I am eternally grateful, Mary.

To my good friend Barbara Echols who read a draft of the book and pointed out places that needed additional information. Barbara read it again after many drafts and again shared her thoughts. After reading it, she encouraged me to get it published and to have the next book be a continuation of the adventures of these characters. Thank you, Barbara.

To Rhoda Fort, an accomplished writer with publications requiring extensive research, who did a thorough critique of this manuscript. Her comments and suggestions were a great help in making me aware of writing style, format, use of senses to draw the reader into the story through characters who experienced the trials and joys of life. Her help was such a learning experience. Thank you, Rhoda.

To my friend Donna Boswell who read the book and edited the final draft. Her comments and suggestions were of great value to me. Thank you, Donna.

Prologue

The story takes place in West Virginia and Kentucky in the late 1920s, initially, then moves forward quickly to life in the late 1940s in the Appalachian Mountains.

The hardships and devastation of the Great Depression and World War II were in the past. People's lives were getting back to normal. Jobs in industry picked up. People felt positive about their future. Even in the depressed coal mining and strip-mining areas of West Virginia life was improving, that is until management began to lay off workers and mining accidents increased. The year was 1947.

Tom Cole operated a large earth moving machine in a strip-mining area of West Virginia. His job had its dangers, but the pay was good. Tom and Flora Cole sometimes lived above their means, and frivolous spending was their downfall, causing them to relocate to the mountains of Appalachia and start a new career in lumbering.

Josephine (Jo) La Russa Graven

Perseverance Road

Josephine (Jo) La Russa Graven

Tough Times

Tom lay in the mud with a fifty-pound steel rail on his left foot, the blood spurting out of it like a fountain, and his leg bone poking up from under the skin. His co-workers heard his cries and put down their railroad ties to run to him. One man took off his flannel shirt and tied it around Tom's foot as a tourniquet. Tom screamed again and pounded the ground. Another burly worker saw Tom in the pool of blood and ran back to get his battered truck. He parked it as close as he could to Tom. Four workers lifted Tom onto the hard, cold bed of the truck. Again, Tom's piercing screams filled the air.

Two of the men climbed on the back of the truck with Tom. They kept talking to him to take his mind off the intense pain. Tom was as pale as a ghost and went in and out of consciousness as they traveled the rutty dirt road toward the hospital. The workman driving cursed each time he hit a pothole and Tom screamed; he bounced up and down as his body slammed back to the gritty steel truck bed.

The driver was blowing his horn, waving his arm up and down, and yelling as the wagon approached the crossroad. The horse and wagon did not stop until it was in the middle of the road, and the truck swerved onto the rocky side of the road, then back on the road. The men in the back of the truck grabbed Tom's arms to keep him from sliding off the truck, and Tom screamed in agony.

The tires were squealing as the truck pulled up to the emergency room entrance. The passenger door flew open and the worker ran inside, yelling he needed help. The nurse at the front desk ran outside with the panicked worker, then ran back in the hospital to get additional help. A few minutes later, two of the hospital staff in scrubs ran out with a gurney and clean towels. They wrapped Tom's bloody foot and moved him to the stretcher. Tom's knotted hands pushed down into the mattress and he again screamed in agony.

*****

Old Shorty, a local, having seen the accident and Tom on the ground, turned and ran to Tom and Flora's duplex, only to find she was not at home. He knew where Tom's mother lived and ran as fast as he could to her farm.

As he entered the long driveway to the house, he began yelling, "Mrs. Cole, Mrs. Cole, Tom's been hurt really bad! They took him to the hospital."

Flora looked to her mother-in-law in a state of panic.

The elder Mrs. Cole said, "Run, Flora. I'll tend the baby."

Flora turned and began to run, leaving Old Shorty bent over trying to catch his breath. It seemed to Flora like it took forever to reach the hospital, with tears streaming down her face.

She ran in, grabbed the nurse coming toward her, and in a choking, crying voice wailed, "My husband! How is my husband? I need to see my husband!"

The nurse wrapped her arms around Flora and let her cry, then pulled back and told her, "Your husband is in surgery. He has a broken leg and a badly mangled left foot. He has lost a lot of blood and is very weak. His foot may have to be amputated. Mr. Cole will be in surgery for hours. My dear, the surgeon is doing everything he can to save his foot."

The nurse calmed Flora down and reassured her Tom would be all right. As she sat by the nurse, an aide brought two cups of coffee, handing one to Flora and one to the nurse. Flora took the cup with shaking hands and just looked at the black liquid.

After a few minutes of silence, the nurse asked, "Do you have family here?"

Flora shook her head, "No, we have only Tom's mother."

She paused for a few minutes, bit her lip then said, "Tom just got the job with the railroad a year ago. He'd have a regular paycheck and could still help his momma on her farm. The next day he rented the duplex, and we

3

were married that evening by a justice of the peace who gave us advice.

"I remember his words. He told us, 'Marriage is a lifetime commitment with trials and joy. Accept them and work together. Share the joys of life as a couple. Depend on each other. Accept the trials and move forward with God's help, prayer, hard work and love.'"

Flora rattled on, "We shared the joys as newlyweds. I continued to work as a clerk at Newberry's and worked there until The Depression. I found myself without a job and pregnant. I made baby clothes out of flannel and muslin scraps my mother-in-law gave me. I gave birth to our son three months ago at home and dressed him in the soft muslin gown. Now this."

Flora broke down and began to cry again. She turned to the nurse, grabbed her hand and asked, "Is my husband going to die?"

The nurse said nothing. Instead, she wrapped her arms around Flora's shoulders and just let her cry some more. She didn't have an answer for Flora.

Hours passed before the doctor came into the waiting room, still in scrubs with spatters of Tom's blood on his shirt.

He knelt down before Flora, put his hands over her hands, and said, "Your husband had a very serious accident that has severely damaged his left foot. I had to set bones in his foot and remove shattered bone. He also had a broken leg that I set before working on his foot. I am concerned about his ability to walk once it heals. He will have to be hospitalized for weeks, possibly even a couple of months. He is heavily sedated and will be until the pain eases. We will keep him in recovery overnight. You won't be able to see him until he is out of recovery tomorrow. Go home, dear, care for your baby and get a little rest. I promise we will let you see him in the morning."

The nurse offered to walk her home, but Flora refused.

In a cracking voice, Flora said, "I need time to think and ask God's help. I'll be all right. Thank you for staying with me."

Flora left the hospital in one direction and the nurse turned and left in the opposite direction. As Flora walked home, she pleaded with God, "Please heal Tom. I need him. Our son needs his father."

Josephine (Jo) La Russa Graven

Return to Consciousness

Before the accident, Tom had worked for the railroad laying track ten hours a day in the mountainous area of West Virginia for expansion of the railroad.

The morphine, ordered by the doctor in charge of his hospital care, kept him in a semi-conscious state for three weeks. Each time he opened his eyes, he saw Flora seated beside his bed and felt the warmth of her hand resting on his arm. He realized she walked six miles each day to be with him.

During the next seven days his mind cleared. He no longer needed morphine to ease the pain. He could wiggle his exposed foot and feel Flora rubbing his toes. He could slide his casted leg and foot from side to side in the bed, but he was still unable to get out of bed.

He repeatedly told the doctor, "I want to go home. I can rest better in my own bed. My wife and mother can be my nurses and do what is done in this hospital."

On Monday of the fifth week, the doctor released him with orders to stay in bed with his foot elevated for three weeks, then use crutches to keep weight off the foot until fully healed. Tom agreed and went home in the same truck that brought him to the hospital.

For seven months he hobbled on crutches. Angered, one day he slung the crutches and mumbled a few curse words as he picked himself up off the ground. The railroad paid the hospital bill and doctor, but didn't continue his wages. Without pay, the move to his mother's house became permanent. The foot was not healing, and he had difficulty walking. The doctor said it would get better over time. Time was something Flora and he didn't have. They needed some income. He hated the thought of Flora having to go back to work, but it might be a necessity.

*****

Flora, determined to find a job to support her family, argued with Tom every day. It would only be a little while until Tom could go back to work. Tom was totally against it. They argued for weeks. Silence followed. Flora left the house after each argument and hurriedly walked until she regained her composure and the tears stopped.

Today was different. Harsh words were said, and both felt the pain they had caused. Flora ran from the house with cheeks red as fire and clenched fists. She didn't stop behind the big oak tree as she had done before. She ran as fast as she could into town and applied for a job at a bread factory.

Tom's mother kept her grandson and cared for Tom. Flora went to work at the Merrimount Bread Company, bagging bread for ten hours each day. They paid twelve cents an hour. The company took advantage of people who were desperate to find a job.

She told herself, "It is only until Tom's foot is healed and he can go back to work."

Flora nursed her son in the morning and pumped milk into a glass jar for his mid-day feeding. As soon as she came home, she nursed him again. When he woke in the middle of the night, she nursed him again. The strain of the long hours left her tired and snappish.

Josephine (Jo) La Russa Graven

She Had Little Time for Him

Tom watched his young wife leave each morning and come home to care for him and their infant son. He hated every day she had to work outside the house. His anger at himself for getting hurt and forcing his wife to work at the bread factory unintentionally caused him to be cross with Flora. She had little time for him, and he resented it. He made a promise to himself. Once he could return to work, he would never let her work outside their home again.

He expected to go back to work at the railroad, but the leg didn't heal correctly, and he was in constant pain. Every morning, he wrapped the foot tightly with tape so he could walk. He walked with a limp and had a foot that turned outward. A spokesman for the railroad told him he couldn't return to work.

Most jobs required a man to be physically able to do heavy manual work. When employers saw Tom's damaged foot, they wouldn't even let him fill out an application. He had to find a job that didn't require him walking.

He'd heard from a friend that the coal industry near his home had started to strip mine for coal. The company had a new mechanical machine for strip mining. Maybe, just maybe, he could get a job driving and operating the mechanical arm. He drove his truck to the coal company's office the morning they were taking applications. There were men standing in front listening to a coal supervisor explain what the job entailed.

Tom sat in his truck for a few minutes. He was despondent as he saw the number of able-bodied men listening to the job requirements. Lacking hope, but determined to find a job, he limped over to hear the last of the offer. Some men left. They didn't know how to operate the machine. Some could not read and couldn't fill out the application.

Tom filled out the application and responded to the supervisor's questions about his ability to operate farm equipment. He stood in front of the supervisor who was sitting at the table with Tom's application in his hands. Tom waited to hear the rejection, but to his surprise, he was hired. Tom spent several hours with his new boss going over the earth moving machine and how to operate it. He would report to work the next day. Pay would be $25 per week.

Tom drove to the bread factory and waited for Flora to come out. He told her the good news and both their spirits lifted. She flung her arms around his neck and just held on to him.

Tom pulled away and said, "I promised myself that when I got a job, you would never have to work outside our home again. I start work tomorrow and will make $25 a week.

"Some of what I make will be saved and someday I will buy you a proper house of our own."

*****

For four years they continued to live with Tom's mother. They had a second child whom they named Allen. With two sons and a wife, they needed a bigger house. He heard of a two-story house that had been abandoned during The Depression. The bank owned it now and had it up for sale. Tom took Flora to the house. They peeked in every window, then sat on the front steps. Tom assured her he could do the work to make it habitable.

He haggled with the banker for an hour about the price. Finally, the banker agreed to sell it for $3,800. Tom put the $600 he had saved as a down payment and signed the papers on the mortgage. The house note would be $45 per month. Tom was earning $120 a month. He reckoned he could make the note and spend a little money on his family.

Tom was smiling when he showed Flora the mortgage papers, then he kissed her.

Promise Kept

Tom and Flora continued to live with his mother for another six months after purchasing the house. He worked on Sunday afternoons repairing warped floors, patching the leaky roof and repairing the chimneys of the two fireplaces. Flora put wintergreen alcohol on his damaged foot and wrapped it with an ace bandage before he put on his boots.

He continued to put money aside each week until he could buy a wood-burning stove for cooking and heat, and an icebox. He made a wood-frame bed for each of his boys. His mother gave them the iron bed they had been using. He built a kitchen table out of wood flats he found on the side of the railroad tracks.

Tom found four odd chairs and a wardrobe at the junk yard. The chairs needed scrubbing before he could paint them. He used a soft worn rag made from an old diaper to wash the wardrobe, then used another diaper rag to rub the paste wax into the scratches. It looked like new when he had finished. He now had enough furniture in the house to move his family into their own home.

Each week Tom put three dollars of his pay in the old toolbox to save for nicer furniture. He did not trust banks, so he had always used the old toolbox as a safe. As he had enough money, Tom and Flora purchased one nice piece of furniture until all their furniture was store bought.

He watched as his sons grew, and decided to fence the yard so they had a safe place to play. He took two old tires, slick from wear, and made swings. He then hung them on thick branches of the massive oak tree in the side yard. He built a ladder on the elm tree so his boys could climb to a wide branch and pretend they were looking for pirate ships or watching for Indians to attack their imaginary fort.

His mind was always racing and wondering how to make the yard even nicer. He bought a small tractor out of the Sears catalogue and each spring he plowed Flora a vegetable garden. He planted roses in the front yard and planted two apple trees in the backyard. The blossoms were snow white in spring and the big juicy red apples made the best jelly, apple butter and apple pies.

She wanted to raise chickens, so he built a coop and purchased twelve chicks and a rooster. They always had eggs and chickens to eat. Tom purchased a rifle and ammunition to hunt for game. With a river nearby, one Christmas he gave his boys fishing poles and lures. Rather than dig for worms, he'd buy a carton of worms whenever his family wanted to fish and picnic. Flora hooked the worms on the lines, and Tom took the fish his sons caught off the lure. Most were too small to keep, but Flora and Tom loved to see the excited facial expressions on their sons' faces and hear their yells of excitement with each catch.

Barber's Dairy offered home delivery of milk, eggs and cheese twice a week. Every Monday morning, they found two quarts of milk, a pound of hoop cheese and a pound of butter on their porch when they got up; and every Thursday morning, two quarts of milk were delivered.

The daily newspaper, thrown by a young boy, bounced in the yard and onto the porch every morning. Tom saved it to read at night after supper as Flora did her knitting, the two boys played checkers, and the family listened to the big bands on the radio, sometimes singing along.

Tom was proud of his ability to provide a nice home and some of the frills of a good life for his family. They went out to eat twice a month and to the movies. He gave Flora money to buy clothes rather than make them. He bought bicycles for the family to ride. Money wasn't a worry. Life was good. He still put money aside, but now in the 1940s he'd opened a savings account. Every week he put three dollars in the savings account as he had done for years. The family spent the rest of his paycheck.

As his sons grew older, he sent them to a summer camp for two weeks and one year even paid for a neighbor's son to attend. He didn't want his boys to do without. His pay increased each year and he was confident that he'd never have to worry about a job as long as there was coal to be mined. The years passed and his sons were nearly grown and in high school. He didn't have a care in the world.

Josephine (Jo) La Russa Graven

Wolf at The Gate

"Tom Cole, could I see you in my office?" his boss asked.

Tom thought he was going to get a raise, but he was wrong, ever so wrong. Others sat outside his boss' office that day and all for the same reason—another layoff. This time he received the pink slip. He had until the end of the month, just two weeks from now, to figure out how to pay the bills and feed his family.

He had given the coal company an honest day's work for his pay. The West Virginia Sentinel News, September 12, 1947, edition said they had a larger than expected profit last quarter. Why the layoff? Fifty-four men out of work in a coal mining town. He pondered how he would break the news to Flora.

Tom didn't say anything when he got home. He went out to the yard and chopped wood for the fireplaces and stacked logs on the side of the fence. They had two fireplaces. They would at least stay warm, that is if the wolf, the banker, didn't come to repossess the house. The coal company supervisor said they'd be back on the job in a few months. They could make it, though it would be tough for a few months. There would be no eating out or movies. They would have to pray nobody got sick or hurt. He put his axe in the tool shed and went in for supper.

As he prepared to say grace, he looked at his wife and two children. They deserved better than this humble existence. The family bowed their heads as Tom said the blessing.

"God bless us for this food to nourish our bodies, and bless us with the nourishment that only You can give to save our souls. Amen."

He watched as his boys went back for seconds of their momma's fried chicken and heaped more potatoes on their plates. He ate only one piece of chicken and took half the potatoes he usually ate. He didn't have an appetite tonight. He knew Flora sensed something was wrong. Hopefully, she thought fatigue and pain in his foot after a day's work and an hour chopping wood caused his drawn face.

As they prepared for bed, Tom told Flora of the layoff.

He said, "We will have to cut back on spending."

They already had a second mortgage on the house. He knew the bank wouldn't be tolerant if he came back again. Tom had already checked the savings account book and knew they had $530.89 in savings. That would pay the bills for a few months.

Flora cried, "We've lived through a depression and a war and just when life gets comfortable this happens. It isn't fair! Tom, it just isn't fair."

He just held her in his arms and whispered, "We have made it this far. We will survive this too."

They just clung to each other for a few minutes as she cried on his shoulder and he rubbed her back. Thankfully, she couldn't see the deep creases on his brow as he wondered how they would make it. His wife fell asleep in his arms with tear stains down her cheeks, but sleep eluded Tom. What if the layoff lasted longer than expected? Why now? The war had ended. The economy had picked up. It just didn't make sense. He stroked her hair as they lay in bed.

*****

Morning came too soon, and with an aching, tired body Tom crawled out of bed. He stoked the fire, then watched as Flora started breakfast and the boys appeared at the breakfast table. Tom sipped on his coffee as Flora put the biscuits, ham and eggs on the table. He blessed the food and told his sons of the layoff as they wolfed down the ham and eggs. They stopped eating as their father spoke.

He told them, "It would be helpful if both of you could get a part-time job."

"No way!" piped Peter, age seventeen. He pushed back his chair and stomped around the room, his eyes glaring, and his fists clenched. "I'm on the football team. When would I work? Are you asking me to give up football?"

Tom stood, "Stop right there! Change that tone of voice. Think of this family, not just your football."

Tom's face was red. He felt the pounding of his heart and the heat of his anger. He walked over to the window and stared at the chickens pecking at stones and scratching for worms until he regained his composure, then sat back down.

Peter sat down but didn't continue to eat his breakfast. Everyone felt tense. Tom rubbed Flora's shoulder as he sat down at the table. He picked up his cup to take a sip of coffee, then put it back down. He wasn't in the mood for food anymore either.

Allen, age fifteen, sat silently as his brother ranted. Now he broke the silence and asked his dad, "You have never asked us to work before. Why now?"

Still red-faced, Tom turned to his younger son. He looked at him and realized how worked up he had been with Peter.

In a calmer voice, he said, "The coal company gave out pink slips yesterday to fifty-four miners, including me. I have two weeks of work, then indefinitely without work. I may have to go elsewhere to find work. We have a house note to pay and a note on my truck. We have a doctor bill for the busted knee you had earlier this month.

"Son, it isn't what I want and, prayerfully, it won't come to that, but we must make changes. Your mother and I have enough in savings to sustain us for a couple of months, but there won't be any eating out or going to the movies. This is a coal mining town, son. In the past, when miners have had a layoff, it has been for a prolonged period of time, not just a few months. I thought operating a strip mining machine it would never happen to me."

Tom did odd jobs for the elderly in the community and made enough to feed his family over the next couple of months, but bills kept piling up. He saw his wife taking in sewing alterations to pay the minimum amount of the doctor bill. His request to his sons had been answered. He was proud of his sons showing responsibility to meet the needs of the family in their own ways.

Allen collected soda bottles and beer bottles to make a little money. Every Saturday morning, he picked up the empty bottles behind Miller's Pub and sold them back to the grocery store for a penny each. He didn't spend any on himself. He gave the money to his mother for food. Tears slid down her face as she hugged her younger son.

Peter continued to play football, but delivered groceries to the elderly on weekends. The money earned help pay for gas for the truck. Meals became sparse. Jars of vegetables and jams Flora had canned the summer before the layoff were quickly being used up.

The day came when Tom had to talk to the banker. He could no longer meet the house note.

Tom asked Mr. Parker at the bank, "Can the bank give me an extension? Can I pay just the interest until I go back to work?"

Mr. Parker said, "For three months you have been late with the house payment. I have been lenient. I know it's tough, but the bank has to survive too."

"Can I refinance what is owed on the house to get a lower payment on the balance?"

"Tom, you don't have a job, nor any prospect of one. The bank can't take such a risk."

Tom's hands were knotted and his head bowed as he tried to accept the disappointing news.

He raised his head, looked Mr. Parker in the eyes and asked, "How long do I have?"

Mr. Parker hesitated and answered Tom, "If you don't make a payment for six months, the bank will have to foreclose on your house."

"Six months—that gives me some hope. Maybe the demand for coal will pick up by then."

Tom pulled his weary body from the chair, extended his hand, thanked Mr. Parker for his time and walked the mile home. He saw Flora get up from the porch swing and wait for him to tell her what Mr. Parker had said. The gloom on his wife's face matched his hopeless spirit.

He held his wife in his arms for a few minutes, pulled away, and told her, "Flora, the bank won't give us an extension on the mortgage. If we can't pay the notes for six months, they will take the house."

Flora cried, "They can't do that. We have been paying on this house for fourteen years. It is all we have, Tom. How will we survive?"

He pulled her into his arms and rubbed her back and told her, "I don't know, honey."

The next day Tom looked at his options. The house note plus the second mortgage was $79.43 per month. The truck note was $49. The doctor bill $11 per month, with three months still owed. The electric bill and water bill together averaged around $21 each month. They needed money for gas and some food. Soon they would have to buy more food as the stock from the summer garden became depleted.

The chickens provided the eggs and what meat they were eating. He didn't have money to buy bullets for his gun, so he couldn't hunt for deer, rabbits, or squirrels, and he couldn't ask his friends to help him anymore. His friends were facing hard times too.

Months passed and he had to trade down on his truck. Luther's Auto let him have a twenty-year-old truck in exchange for his half-paid truck. He had to continually tinker with it to keep it running, but he had to cut their monthly expenses.

Mr. Parker had the foreclosure sign in his hand as he started to knock on the door just as Tom opened it. He invited Mr. Parker to come inside. Tom pleaded with him to give them more time. Mr. Parker listened, but kept shaking his head *No*. Flora was sitting on the edge of the sofa, biting her bottom lip to keep from crying. She could not hold back the tears. Her body began to shake and her loud sobs and a pleading look tore at Mr. Parker's heart. He gave them a few more months, but warned the next time he came, he'd foreclose.

And then the day came when the black sedan pulled up in front of the house and put the foreclosure sign in front of the gate. They had a month to leave. They had lost it all.

In Search of a Job

Flora packed two sandwiches and a thermos of coffee as she did every morning for her husband. She watched as Tom poured himself another cup of coffee and drank it as he looked out the kitchen window. He just stared at the yard. As he put down his cup, she dried her wet hands and went to him. Tom put out his arm and pulled her close to him.

He stroked her hair and whispered, "I'll be back by dark, don't worry, honey. God won't let us down. Pray for us as you work around the house today."

She stood at the front door and watched her husband limp down the path to the gate. Tears slid down her face as she watched her hunch-shouldered husband open the gate and wave. The layoff had robbed them of the happiness they had always shared through the years and replaced it with constant worry.

She turned and surveyed the house. She went from room to room looking for anything else they could sell.

They'd sold the piano Granny Tully had left her. She recalled the laughter as a child singing gospel songs in the evening. Granny played the piano and granddaddy played the fiddle. It was one of the few happy memories she had of living with them after her daddy died. Her brother Clyde got the fiddle when Granddaddy died. Then Momma died of tuberculosis the next year.

Flora ran her hand across the pine hutch her daddy had made. She couldn't sell it. The sight of it reminded her of him. The hutch held the flowered dishes her mother-in-law gave them the day she and Tom married. She opened the slender drawer and saw the album of family pictures, yellowed with age.

She sat at the kitchen table and slowly turned the pages as she sipped the last of her cold coffee. She paused as she looked at the picture of Granddaddy and Granny Tully with their two children playing in the yard. She wondered if the cabin still existed or had it been devoured by kudzu.

Flora sighed as she picked up the picture of Momma and Daddy beside a 1920 Ford. Beneath the picture someone had written the word *someday*. She ran her finger over the shape of the word and more tears fell.

Daddy died in a mining accident that year. Momma had to give up the company-owned house after he died. Momma wrote her father, and he came with his pickup truck to get Momma, her brother, Clyde, and her. They moved in with Granny and Granddaddy for a few years until Momma got a job in Huntington at a mining office as a clerk.

Life was different at her grandparents. Houses were far apart and there were few children as playmates. They had an outhouse instead of an indoor toilet. The one-room school had young students and students in upper grades taller than the teacher. She felt she had been torn away from all she had ever known and loved.

Thinking back on her childhood, she opened the envelope with curls of Peter and Allen's baby hair. She rubbed the hairs between her fingers as she looked up at the ceiling and wailed, "Lord, don't let my boys live as I did as a child."

Flora whimpered as she put the curls back in the envelope then closed the album and left it on the table.

She rinsed her empty coffee cup then folded the patchwork quilt her mother-in-law made for their bed when they married. Flora recalled how happy she and Tom were the day they married. She pulled the quilt up to her chest then rubbed her cheek with the worn coverlet. She draped it across the sofa and looked around to see what to do next.

She felt lost in her own home, so many of the small objects they'd collected through the years had been sold. The small end table no longer held the radio. It had been sold for $5 to a local used furniture store. The radio now sat on the mantel above the fireplace.

She stoked the fire in the wood-burning stove before climbing down to the root cellar for a cabbage, potatoes, an onion, and a few carrots to make a pot of soup. She took an accounting of the vegetables: one bin of potatoes, eight cabbages, several bunches of collards, a handful of carrots, onions and turnip roots. She balanced the cabbage, potatoes and carrots in one corner of her apron and closed the root cellar as she heard her neighbor Lois' voice.

"Billy Harold caught a mess of fish this morning, more than we can eat. Can you use this string of fish?"

Lois put the fish in a pan of water near the sink as she spoke.

Flora put down the vegetables she had in her folded apron and gave her neighbor a hug. It had been a week since they had any meat. Flora filled two glasses with water and handed one to Lois as they sat at the kitchen table. She had nothing else she could share.

"Sit a spell, Lois. I could use a little company today. I feel so helpless. I've sold everything we don't absolutely need."

Lois took a sip of her water, set the glass down and asked, "Tom had any luck finding a job?"

Flora shook her head. "Nothing. He goes out every morning looking for work, but nobody is hiring. Some days he is picked up at the corner heading out of town as a day laborer and earns $5, and some days he can't find any work. If he can't find a job, we can't pay the house note. We have missed three already. If we miss three more, the bank will foreclose on the house. It is hopeless, Lois. The mining company has laid off fifteen more men. Some of them are going in the mines to dig coal. Tom promised me he wouldn't. Every few months there is another mining accident. I lost my daddy and my brother, Clyde, in mining explosions."

Lois asked, "If you can't meet the house note, when would you have to move?"

"We have until July 15th. Mr. Parker gave us a little extra time so Allen and Peter could finish the school year and Peter could graduate.

"I think Mr. Parker hopes the mining company will end the layoff and Tom will be back to work. Then he can refinance the balance owed on the house and set up a plan to make the back payments. He doesn't want to see us lose the house. Mr. Parker said the bank will give us $100 if it has to foreclose. We have no money, Lois. That $100 is all we'd have to find another place to live and that will only pay a few months' rent."

Flora took a sip of water and swallowed hard to keep from crying. She turned to face Lois again and said, "For fourteen years we have paid on this house, and we have only $100 to show for it."

Lois got up, put her arms around Flora and just held her tight, but said nothing. A few moments passed before Flora quit crying and freed herself from Lois' arms, wiped her eyes and said, "I'm okay, Lois. This is just hard to believe and accept."

Lois asked, "What is Peter going to do after graduation?"

Flora's hands were clasped together as she answered, "He has always dreamed of going to college. It's a dream that won't come true now."

Flora sat down, put her hands over her eyes and cried. In a choking voice she said, "He asked his boss at the grocery store if he could work more hours this summer, but that doesn't look promising."

Lois reached for Flora's hands and asked, "Is there anything I can do?"

"You share your food," as she pointed to the pan of fish, "and you are my sounding board," Flora said, as she ran her hand across her brow.

Lois picked up the album that sat on the table and began to leaf through the pages.

She asked, "Who is this?"

Flora replied, "My granny and granddaddy."

"Is this their cabin?"

"Yes, we had to live with them for a few years after my daddy died in a mining accident."

Lois was curious and asked, "Where is it?"

Flora put her hand on the album then turned to Lois and said, "It's above a hollow in eastern Kentucky. The log cabin is deep in the woods. To get to the cabin we had to wind up the mountain until we spotted the planks fuzzy with moss. Granddaddy put the planks down when we moved there, so we could find our way to the cabin."

Lois asked, "Have you been there since they died?'

"No, my brother, Clyde, took his truck and took Momma to get the piano, the fiddle and a few pieces of furniture. All of it was made by my daddy or granddaddy."

Lois stood and said, "Well, honey, I got to go. Billy Harold will be looking for me."

She patted Flora's hand and said, "You hang in there. God's got a plan. He's just testing your faith. Better times are coming."

Flora took her big spoon and scraped the scales off the fish then removed the bones and guts. As she worked, she thought about what Lois had said, "God is testing your faith."

Flora wondered why she had looked at that album. Was the answer in those pages? She washed her hands, opened the album and stared at the cabin. Was this cabin part of God's plan of where to live?

As she put the album back in the hutch, she saw her sons racing through the yard and bounding through the kitchen door, laughing. It lifted her spirits to see her sons so happy. Both gave their momma a hug and threw their books down on the table. She could tell they had a good day at school.

Josephine (Jo) La Russa Graven

Unexpected News

The sky was gray with the smell of rain as Peter and Allen left for school that April morning. It matched their mood. They talked about the changes happening at home. Dad without a job, the need for them to find part-time jobs, and no dinners out or movies until their dad had a job. Peter regretted his outburst of temper at the breakfast table the morning their dad asked them to get part-time jobs. He'd apologized to his dad. His dad said that morning that he had been thinking only of himself, that he had to accept this harsh truth. His dream of college no longer existed.

Peter's somber mood changed as the two brothers entered the school ground. Peter put his books down beside the big oak tree and joined his buddies as they played touch football. Allen caught up with his girlfriend Patsy, and they reviewed material for the history test they would have. When the morning bell rang, everyone hurried to their lockers and to class.

As Peter entered first period, Mr. Herman, his English teacher, handed him a note from Mrs. Mixon, the school counselor. Peter walked to his desk wondering what he had done that required him to get a note from Mrs. Mixon.

The slip of paper said, "Come to my office at your study hall time."

He had study hall third period. He thought, *it must not be too serious, if she doesn't want to see me until then.* He folded the note and put it in his blue jeans pocket. After second period, he walked to her office and knocked on the door.

"Come in!" she called.

Peter took a seat in front of her desk and asked, "Have I done something wrong?"

Mrs. Mixon chuckled and said, "No, Peter. I want to talk to you about something else. Peter, I checked your records as I do for every student who is about to graduate. I found A's and B's in all your classwork. Comments made by your teachers each year indicate you are excellent in math and science. You are the kind of student who would excel in college. I am aware that your father lost his job. That is why I've looked over all the college brochures I received to see the best college for our students. I found a college near here that…"

Peter popped out of his chair and headed for the door. He said, "Yes, a college that 'fits', but my parents don't have the money to send me, so forget it."

Mrs. Mixon said, "Sit down, Peter. Listen to what I am about to tell you."

Peter turned and slammed back in the chair. Belligerently, he said, "Fat chance you have a way for me to go to college."

He slouched in the chair and began hitting his fist into his other hand. His face was as red as a beet and his jaw tight.

Mrs. Mixon said nothing until he looked at her. She shared, "Peter, there is a college not far from here in Blyne, Kentucky, that allows students to work their way through college. You would live in college housing and work for a business or individual in the area. The money earned would be paid to the college for your tuition, books, fees, housing and meals. You would be putting yourself through college.

"I have a brochure from the college that I would like you and your parents to read. I'd like your parents and you in my office at 8 a.m. Friday morning. Are you interested?"

Peter sat there for a couple of minutes to let the conversation register in his mind, then asked, "I'd work and they pay the bills for my college?"

Mrs. Mixon nodded and put the brochure out for Peter to take.

Peter sat there and reached for the brochure. He started to leave and turned around and faced Mrs. Mixon. In a soft voice he said, "I am sorry for my outburst of temper. It's just everything in our lives has changed and it creates tension for all of us. Forgive me, Mrs. Mixon. Thank you for caring."

He left her office and went to his fourth-period class. He had a difficult time staying focused in his classes that afternoon.

Peter didn't share the news with his brother that afternoon. He'd share with all his family at the supper table. He greeted his mother in a cheery voice and said he had some reading to do before supper. He went into his room and closed the door. Flora nodded and continued to cook, while Allen went outside to do chores.

*****

At dusk Tom opened the door and smiled, though puzzled by the laughter. He leaned down and kissed Flora and saw the sheen in her eyes he hadn't seen in months. He smiled and kissed her again.

He commented, "It smells good in here. Who caught the fish?"

Flora looked up at her husband and replied, "Billy Harold. Lois brought them over and we had girl talk."

Tom put his black lunch pail by the sink and rinsed out his thermos. He handed his wife the $5 he'd earned that day, as he pulled out a chair and sat down for supper. Peter asked to say the blessing as they joined hands. As the family ate, Peter mentioned the brochure Mrs. Mixon had given him.

He told them, "It is a way for me to work my way through college. My work would pay for lodging, tuition, books, fees and meals. The school is in eastern Kentucky. I've read the brochure. She wants you to read it, and

Mom, Dad and I are to meet with her Friday morning at 8 a.m."

Peter handed the brochure to his dad. Tom put down his fork and perused the tri-fold brochure. He handed it to Flora as his worried look became a smile. Flora looked at the cover but wanted Peter to tell her what it said, rather than read it herself. Peter spent a half hour telling his mother what the brochure said, while they sat at the table and finished supper.

*****

Friday morning the whole family walked to the school. Mrs. Mixon waited for them at the front door of the school. Peter introduced them and the counselor shook their hands. She invited Mr. and Mrs. Cole to her office and asked them to have a seat.

She asked, "Have you read the brochure?"

Tom replied, "Yes, we have."

Mrs. Mixon said, "I have been in contact with the admissions office of Blyne College and told them about Peter. The director of admissions seemed very impressed and excited about the possibility of Peter attending Blyne. Of course, I need to fill out the paperwork and mail it to the college admissions office. Once they examine the paperwork and school transcript, they will make their decision and notify me. I must have your permission to send the application. As the brochure stated, Peter would work, and his pay would cover all related costs. It is a scholarship. Do you have any questions?"

Again, Tom responded. "If I understand you and the brochure, all of Peter's college expenses will be covered by his working and attending classes at the same time. When would he have time to study, if he must work when he is not in class? When would he have time to mingle with other students?"

Mrs. Mixon addressed his concerns. "Each semester he will have scheduled classes. He will take thirteen hours his first semester and sixteen hours each semester after that. His job will be on days he has no classes or just one class. He will work twenty hours a week. This schedule will give him ample time to study and take part in school activities or social events. Do you have any other questions?"

Peter asked, "How long will it take before you know if I am accepted?"

She smiled and said, "I should know within a week after they receive your application. They have promised to call me. They will also mail a letter of acceptance to your home. Do you want to go, Peter?"

"YES!"

"Mr. and Mrs. Cole, do I have your permission to complete and mail Peter's application?"

Tom and Flora both said, "Yes."

Peter jumped from his chair and hugged both his parents, then Mrs. Mixon.

Mrs. Mixon said, "I'll let you know when I hear from the college."

Forgotten Cabin

The night after learning Peter might get a scholarship to go to college, the family celebrated with a custard pie Flora had made. After rinsing the plates and forks, Tom and Flora went on the porch and sat on the swing. They felt the cool breeze and listened to the rustling leaves. Flora didn't speak. She let her husband push the swing with his foot and rest his arm on her shoulder. She had something on her mind, but she didn't know how to share it with Tom.

Flora turned toward Tom and said, "Tom, Lois made a comment the other day that I haven't been able to get out of my mind. She said, 'God has a plan. He is just testing your faith.' Then Peter brought home the brochure about college and we met with Mrs. Mixon this morning. Has God been testing our faith?"

Flora continued, "The day Peter brought home the brochure, I'd been looking at the family album and had left it on the table. Lois looked through the pictures and asked about my grandparents' cabin. I inherited it when Momma died."

Tom stopped the swing and looked at Flora in disbelief. "WHAT? You own your grandparents' cabin? You never mentioned that to me! Why not?"

"No, I never did. I pushed it out of my mind so I wouldn't have to remember how hard life there had been. When my dad died, we had to move from the only house I'd ever known and all my friends. I'd only met my grandparents the few times my dad drove up to Breathitt Mountain to see them. Momma became very quiet after my dad died. She had lost her spouse and became very depressed. Though my grandparents did everything they could to make us happy, everything we'd known had changed.

"The cabin had four rooms and it sat on a plot of land deep in the woods. Few children lived nearby. Clyde and I had to attend a one-room schoolhouse with grades one to eight. The students talked funny and dressed differently. At first, they wouldn't play with me at recess. They would spread out at the lunch table, so that left no space for me. Sometimes, when I first started school there, they would knock my books off my desk or trip me as I walked to my desk.

"The school didn't have a bathroom. We had to go in the outhouse to go to the bathroom. I thought spiders or snakes might be in there, and I tried not to go, if I could hold it. Clyde and I had to walk halfway down the mountain to catch the school bus. No one would let us in the seat beside them. We always had to walk to the very back of the bus, and we sat on the metal boxes over the bus wheels. We felt every bump and bounced off the metal boxes sometime.

"Awful, awful change from our lives before moving there, and I hated the change. I just wanted to block out that memory once Momma got the job in Huntington. I never went back there, and I hoped kudzu had swallowed it up."

In Search of the Cabin

Tom turned off the lamp as they climbed into bed. Flora's explanation of the cabin had exhausted her, yet relaxed her. She had shared the anxious feeling she'd had of the cabin and her childhood memories of living there. She felt relaxed because talking about it freed her to know it might be the answer to where they could live, if it hadn't been devoured by the massive strangling vine. Tom held his wife close and could feel her relax on his shoulder and he could feel her breathe.

Tom couldn't sleep thinking about that cabin. Did it still exist? Where would he go to find property records? Flora said Eastern Kentucky. She mentioned Breathitt Mountain and logging. Those were few clues to find a cabin deep in the woods in a state he knew nothing about. If he could locate the plot of land, and it had a livable cabin on it, then it would solve their most pressing problem.

The next morning after breakfast, Tom picked up his lunch pail and thermos, gave Flora a kiss but said nothing of his plans for the day. His steps seemed quicker. He held his head higher with shoulders squared as he opened the gate and waved to Flora, then climbed in the truck and drove off.

Tom didn't go to the corner as usual where day laborers waited to be picked up for a job. He went to the Grayson County Courthouse in Pineyville, Kentucky. He parked in front of the courthouse and prayed he'd chosen the county where the cabin was located. He walked up the white stone steps and pulled open the heavy glass door. Directly in front of him, he saw a large curved desk with a young lady reading the morning paper. She looked up, and in a cheery voice asked if she could help him.

He asked, "Where would I find property records?"

The receptionist said, "Go down that hall," as she pointed to her left, "and turn right at the end of the hall. It is the second room on the right."

Tom entered the room filled with shelves of thick binders and a musty smell. He saw the woman replacing a ledger on a low shelf and cleared his throat to get her attention.

The thin woman, with curly gray hair and deep crow's feet at her eyes, turned toward him and asked, "May I help you, sir?"

Tom said, "I hope so. My wife inherited her grandparents' cabin located somewhere near Majestic, Kentucky, and Breathitt Mountain. I need to find the property record for Ezekiel and Ester Tully."

The clerk asked, "Where did you say the property was located and who did you say were the owners?"

Tom said, "It is on Breathitt Mountain. My wife mentioned a place called Buck's Hollow."

She looked him in the eyes and in a serious voice asked, "And who did you say you are?"

He replied, "Tom Cole."

She continued to question him, "What is your wife's name?"

"My wife's name is Flora, Flora Meeker Cole."

She asked another question to make sure she knew which record book to give him. "And she is the granddaughter of Ezekiel and Ester Tully?"

Tom nodded, then said, "Yes, ma'am."

Tom watched as the records clerk left the counter and went to the stacks behind her desk. He watched as she thumbed her way from book to book, then lifted a heavy ledger and brought it to the counter.

She said, "Mr. Cole, I need to see some form of identification before I can give you this ledger."

Tom pulled out his wallet, took out his license and gave it to her. She looked at the picture on his license and then at him. She pushed the big book toward him and said, "It should be in this book. You can find it by name and location. You can sit at that table by the window."

Tom carried the ledger to the table and said a silent prayer that he'd find it in this book. He searched every page for Tully. He looked for Meeker. He looked for Buck's Hollow and found it.

The description said, "Four-acre parcel of land on the east side of Breathitt Mountain and half mile off County

Road 17 and six miles below Majestic, Kentucky." He wrote down the description, returned the book to the clerk and asked, "How far is it to Majestic, Kentucky?"

As she pulled the ledger close to her, she replied, "It is about twenty-one miles north of here. Are you sure you want to go up there? It is a really depressed area. There are lots of stills in those woods. Those mountain men don't like strangers snooping around. It could be very dangerous for you."

Tom thanked her for her help and advice then left. He sat in his truck and ate his peanut butter sandwiches. He debated whether to go up there today, or tomorrow when he would have the whole day. He decided tomorrow would be a better choice.

He pulled over on the side of the road as he drove home, walked up a slope where wildflowers swayed in the breeze. He picked a handful and put them in his lunch pail. They would bring a smile to Flora's face. He missed her smiles.

*****

After the boys were in bed, Tom showed Flora the property description. He asked her to share landmarks that could help him locate the cabin. He listened and wrote notes as she told him of the zigzagged narrow road with a drop-off on the left and the mountain hugging the road on the right. She said it was a logging road and full of potholes.

He took the family album from the pine hutch and opened it to the picture of her grandparents standing in front of the cabin with its moss-covered planks. Tom told her he would drive there the next day and see if he could find the cabin. He hoped the enormous weeds had not devoured it.

Tom arrived and found a cleared spot with fuzzy moss. He parked the truck as close as he could to the mountain side and walked over to the moss-covered planks. He moved one of the planks over just a little, then walked back to his truck. He drove his truck onto the planks and parked.

Tom saw it all. He could see the tall grasses and weeds, wildflowers, a snakeskin, and could hear the hum of bees and the chatter of birds. He took a sling blade from the back of the truck and cut a path as he searched for the cabin.

The log cabin had not been devoured by kudzu, but needed repairs to make it livable. The door hinges, frozen with rust, would not yield to his tugging. He found a squirrel's nest wedged in the rafters by a broken window. He heard squealing noises of some small creatures who had made the wood-burning stove their home. A white coat of dust covered all surfaces. He noticed the chinking needed repair. The glass in all the windows would need replacing, and all the windowsills had rotted over time. He could not tell if the tin roof, covered with pine straw, leaked. He didn't see any damage other than the windowsills. While the cabin needed a lot of repairs, he thought it livable.

*****

That night after supper, Tom and Flora sat down with their boys and told them.

Their dad said, "Your momma inherited your great grandparents' cabin when they died. It means we have a place to live when we have to move. It is deep in the woods in eastern Kentucky, about forty miles from here.

"It means you will have to change schools, Allen. It is not as nice as this house, but we have no other choice. It means you will have to leave all your friends and make friends with the boys and girls on the mountain. You may have problems adjusting to their way of life. They may resent the fact that you have nicer clothes and speak differently than their dialect.

"We have lost this house and we don't have money to rent one here. It is not what we want, but it is all we have at this moment."

Both boys were silent. They could see the weariness in their parents' body language and understood they had no choice.

Allen asked, "How will I get to school and will they have the same level of classes as I have in my present high school?"

Tom put his hand on his son's shoulder, shook his head, and said, "I don't know."

Peter asked, "Dad, what will you do for a living in the mountains of Kentucky?"

Again, Tom said, "I don't know. All I really know is we have a place to live debt free. The four acres will provide for a large garden and the chickens will provide us with eggs and meat. A pond is on the property and a tributary of the Kentucky River within a mile of the cabin. Both would provide food for us. I can hunt for wild game."

Peter asked, "If it is in the deep woods and no city nearby, how safe will it be?"

"There are stills in the woods. Bootleggers don't like outsiders. We will have to take extra precautions until they learn your mother's family lived there all their lives. They won't accept us at first because we are city folks. We speak differently, dress better and have things like your mother's wringer washer that they can't afford. The cabin needs muscle to fix it; it's been vacant for many years."

Tom shared, "Your momma had to live there for a few years after her daddy died. She only told me of the cabin a few days ago. Your mother's friend, Lois, asked her about the picture of the cabin in the family album that your mother had on the table. Your mother remembered she inherited it after her mother died. She told me about the cabin as we sat on the swing, the night we celebrated the possibility of Peter going to college. I drove to the Grayson County, Kentucky, courthouse, found the property record, and went up the next day to see if I could find it."

Tom told them of finding the moss-covered planks, the tall grass and high weeds. He shared the snakeskin, the buzz of bees, and the birds singing.

He said, "I took my sling blade and cut a path to the cabin. Kudzu hangs from some of the trees, and a little on the side of the cabin. I pulled what kudzu I could off the cabin and hanging low on some trees. There are boards on the porch that need nailing. The steps will have to be replaced. The tin roof is intact. I found no water stains inside the cabin. The glass in the windows is broken. The windowsills are rotten. I can make new ones. There are small creatures living in the wood-burning stove."

Tom laughed when Flora shivered and his son's eyes got very large at the mention of creatures in the stove. He continued, "We will let you boys chase them out of the stove. It will require muscle to get it presentable. I thought we could go up there Sunday after early church service and start to clear part of the yard and work on the cabin before we are forced to leave this house. It will give you a chance to see the area and the cabin."

Tom was very serious when he went over what they needed to accomplish on the first trip to the cabin.

He said to Flora, "You, my dear, will need to show me where the spring pipe is for water. I need to make sure it is flushed, so there is no rust in the line. At some point, your grandparents had indoor plumbing installed. You won't have to use the outhouse."

Tom chuckled. "My dear wife, your job will be to sweep the years of dirt and dust away and wipe down the shelving in the kitchen. I knocked down the deserted squirrel's nest when I first went to the cabin."

Flora served the apple pie Lois had brought over the day before, as Tom finished his conversation about Sunday's trip to the cabin. He drank his cup of coffee and finished his pie as the boys polished off the rest of the pie and milk.

Tom became very serious and said, "I saw smoke from stills and the glint of shotgun barrels as I came up the mountain, and I saw some very unsavory characters peeking out from behind trees. I want us off the mountain before it starts to get dark."

Tom could not turn his mind off. He thought of one thing after another that needed work.

"We have three weeks here and possibly you'll be going to college, so I want you to spend as much time as you can with your friends. It will be a tough adjustment for both of you. Do things you enjoy best. I'd like to stay here until we have to leave."

Tom looked at his wife and said, "We need to look at all the things we still have in the house and how we can pack it all in the truck. Let Lois help you. Give her anything we don't absolutely need. I need to take down the fencing and make a chicken coop to put in the back of the truck for the chickens.

Allen, you can help me take the beds down on the morning of the move. I've asked Bill, Lois' husband, to help me with the heavy hutch and the wringer washer. I have already filled the two gas cans to take with us. I have been trying to think of everything that must be done, and my head keeps reminding me of more to do."

As the days ticked away, Tom thought of other measures they should take before moving. He picked up some empty cardboard boxes from the grocery store. He gave Flora $20 and told her to go to the store and get a few staples to take with them. Tom read over her list: flour, yeast, baking powder, coffee, sugar, lard, powdered milk, salt, pepper, canned meat, peanut butter, Clorox, toilet paper, candles, matches, nails, detergent and soap.

He nodded and said, "We can make it, with God's help."

Can't Turn Back Now

Flora gathered the eggs and made biscuits for breakfast as her husband and sons got ready. She packed three lunches and lined them up on the counter by the side door of the kitchen while the biscuits baked.

Tom came out first and poured himself a cup of coffee. Flora took that as a cue to scramble the eggs and set the table. Peter and Allen seemed in a hurry and wolfed down their breakfast, then disappeared to brush their teeth and grab their books. They wanted to get to school early to have time with their friends before the morning bell rang.

Flora stayed at the table and enjoyed another cup of coffee with Tom. Her husband put his hand over her hand and they turned toward each other and smiled. They sat there, hand in hand, and waited for their boys to come out of the bathroom.

There had been an intense conversation the night before about the move that left their sons anxious. They didn't want to move, but they had no choice. They had no other place to live. They were less stressed this morning, knowing they had a place to live, though primitive.

The $100 the bank gave them when it foreclosed on the house would go a long way toward repairing the porch and buying staples to sustain them until a garden could be planted and harvested. Flora and Tom worried about Allen's adjustment in a new school in Appalachia. His whole world would change. Peter would be in a new environment, but so would all the other freshmen at college.

Peter raced through the kitchen and snatched his lunch off the counter before he said goodbye to his parents. Allen came out of his room a few minutes later, gave his momma a hug and picked up his lunch.

Tom said, "Have a good day."

He turned, smiled and said, "You too, Dad."

Peter was outside pitching rocks, wondering when his little brother would come outside. He had two more weeks in school and wanted to spend them with his friends. His life would change soon, if accepted at college. He'd have to make new friends, work as he attended classes, study, and do it without family. He wouldn't see his family often and when he did it would be for short periods of time. He wanted to be treated as an adult, but the prospects of adulthood and being on his own frightened him. There would be no one to tell him if he were making the right decision.

A stone whizzed past Peter and he turned to see his little brother.

Allen yelled, "Dad said to do your best today."

Peter turned and waved to his parents as the brothers hurried out of the yard. As they walked, Allen asked Peter, "Will you start college this summer or this fall?"

Peter replied, "I don't know if I will get into college. Mrs. Mixon said she'd talk to me after she hears from Blyne College. It's scary. I've never been away from home except to go to summer camp, and I had you and some friends with me. But there's no turning back. Mrs. Mixon has sent the paperwork, and she believes I'm qualified. It means Momma and Dad will have one less mouth to feed."

Allen jokingly replied, "And I won't have you at home to tease me. With Momma, Dad, and me living in the mountains our whole world will turn upside down. It isn't what I ever expected and definitely not what I would have done, if I had a choice."

As they entered the school grounds, Peter dropped his books and lunch bag, and sailed in the air to catch the football intended for his friend Matt. There were thuds and groans as they tumbled to the ground.

Allen left his brother playing touch football and walked to the school steps, where his girlfriend, Patsy, and he always met. He sat down beside her, and they both smiled. Patsy overheard her mother say the Cole family would move in mid-July. She knew his dad had been out of work for nearly a year and asked if he got a job elsewhere. "Is it true?"

Allen replied, "Yes, we are moving. No, my dad doesn't have a job elsewhere. My parents lost the house.

We are moving to a hollow near Majestic, Kentucky, and will live in my great-grandparents' cabin."

Patsy asked, "Is it as nice as your home is here?"

Allen shook his head and said, "No, my dad checked it and said it isn't in good shape, but it is sturdy and has a tin roof that doesn't leak. We drove up there Sunday after early church service. Dad used a sling blade to knock down the high grass and weeds to the cabin.

"Momma swept the inside of the cabin and went from room to room and stood in the door. I think she thought about living there as a child. She had Peter and I clean out the wood-burning stove and chase the little mice out of the house. It is a four-room cabin. At least we have a home.

"Peter is hoping he gets into college, so he said there would be one less mouth to feed. If he gets into college, all the cost of college will be paid by his working as he attends.

"As we were driving up to the cabin, we saw some people living in cardboard houses covered with plastic held down by rocks. Momma said it gets really cold there in winter, and they have snow. I don't know what those people do in winter."

Concerned, Patsy asked, "Will it be safe to live up there?"

Allen answered, "There are bootleggers in the hills. If we don't disturb them or their stills, we should be safe. We will have to be very careful and take our chances. The bank owns the house, and we have no other place to go and no money. It has four acres of land, so we will have a big garden. It is surrounded by woods, so deer, rabbits, squirrels and wild turkey are plentiful. We saw fish jumping in the Kentucky River tributary that is about a mile away. Momma is taking her chickens. We scouted the grounds and saw wild berries, mushrooms and dandelions for poke salad. Spring water has been piped to the house, and it has a bathroom."

The morning bell rang. They stood and started to walk into the school as Peter ruffled his brother's hair and said, "Patsy, what do you see in this little brother of mine? No smooching on the stairwell. That's for the moonlight."

Allen's face turned crimson and Patsy looked down, then sideways at Allen. Peter ducked in his classroom and sat down, still grinning. He had teased his little brother again. Then his face changed to a frown as he realized he'd miss this playfulness if he went to college.

*****

Peter was near the top of the stairs between classes when he heard his name called. He turned around and saw Mrs. Mixon at the bottom of the steps. Hesitantly, he asked, "Mrs. Mixon, did you hear from the college?"

Mrs. Mixon had a big smile on her face when she replied, "Yes, I did."

Peter started back down the steps, "Did I get in?"

The counselor nodded her head to indicate yes and spoke, "Yes, and there is more. Come by my office after school and I will explain. Go to your class before you are late."

Puzzled, Peter walked back up the stairs and kept looking back to see Mrs. Mixon, but she had disappeared into the crowd of students. The rest of the school day, Peter had a hard time focusing in class. He kept looking at the clock, wanting the last bell to ring. He kept wondering, *What more could there be? Would this day ever end, so he could go to her office to find out?*

Peter hurried to Allen's locker as he darted out of class to let his brother know he had to see Mrs. Mixon before he could go home. They raced down the steps. Allen sat down on the floor and did his algebra homework. Peter knocked on the counselor's office door and entered.

She looked up from the folders she had before her and told him to have a seat. She paused for a minute with a smile on her face. Peter moved to the edge of the chair and waited for her to speak.

"Peter, the college is offering you a scholarship to attend Blyne for four years. As I told you earlier, you will work twenty hours a week and take thirteen credit hours the first semester. All your college expenses will be paid by the scholarship. You will receive $5 a month spending money.

"The college has acquired another home to use as student quarters. This house needs painting and a few repairs. The college wants to know if you would be willing to come mid-July and work with a maintenance man. You would live in the house being repaired. You would be paid $75 for the six weeks of work. There will be four incoming freshmen working on the house. Are you interested?"

"Yes, ma'am!"

Allen stood as the door to Mrs. Mixon's office opened. Peter bounded out the door, grabbed his little brother, and they danced around. On the way home, he told Allen of the scholarship, the spending money, and the summer job.

His parents were sitting at the kitchen table going over the list of what needed to be done before the move.

Peter couldn't contain himself when he saw them through the window. He burst in the front door and blurted out, "I got a full scholarship, will get $5 a month spending money, and a summer job repairing and painting the house where I will be living. I will make $75. I report to the college on July 15th."

He grabbed his mother from her chair and they danced around the kitchen, as his dad laughed at the sight of his wife and son moving around the kitchen floor. He gave his son a hug and told him how proud he was of him.

Josephine (Jo) La Russa Graven

Peter Leaves for College

During the weeks before Peter left for college in mid-July, his mother checked the buttons on his shirts, knitted him four pairs of socks and promised to have a new sweater made before winter. Peter watched as his mother scurried around the house trying to send him off with clean, mended clothes, a warm quilt she'd made many years before, and some of her homemade candy and cookies. He knew she didn't want to see him leave, so this was her way of letting go, yet keeping him close.

The morning he left, his momma made a big breakfast of scrambled eggs, pancakes, sausage and milk. He finished his last swallow of milk and took his plate and glass to the sink. His momma stood and waited for him to turn around and come into her outstretched arms. They stood there for a few minutes not saying anything. His mother stepped back and turned away, so he couldn't see her tears. She cleared her throat and wiped her eyes, picked up the tin of cookies and homemade candy, and put it in a paper bag.

She stood there with the bag in one hand and said, "Peter, you know how to be a gentleman, so I expect you to be one. Study the books, not the girls, at that school."

"Momma, do you think I would play around rather than study?"

She looked up to her tall son and put her hands on her hips before answering,

"'Given the opportunity and no parent to keep you in check, yes I do."

Peter went over to his mother and put his arms around her and held her close. Peter felt excited about going to college but sad about leaving his family for long periods of time. He didn't expect to see them until Christmas break.

Flora took a small bag from her pocket and handed it to Peter. She didn't look up for fear of crying and said, "Some stamps, writing paper, and postcards." And almost in a whisper said, "Drop a line once a week, son. I'd feel better knowing how you are." His face lit up with a smile and he promised to write.

His dad appeared at the door and looked at his watch. Peter knew it was time to leave. He looked around the kitchen, gave his momma a kiss, and ran his hand through his brother's hair, then climbed into his dad's battered truck. As they pulled out of the yard, his mother wiped tears from her eyes and put her arm around her younger son.

*****

As his dad drove, Peter watched the woods, listened to the sounds of nature and observed the serious look on his father's face. There was an unspoken need for silence as they descended the hills and headed for the highway and the hardware store where the Trailways bus stopped. His dad parked the truck and they talked while they waited for the bus.

"Son, you have the opportunity to make something of yourself. People believe in you, just as your mother and I do. Mrs. Mixon has gone out of her way to make sure you go to college. Don't waste it, son. There is a time for playfulness and a time to be serious. I don't mean you can't have fun while in college. What I am trying to say is, do your best. That is all your mother and I ask of you. You are smart, and if you are determined, nothing will prevent you from reaching your dreams."

Peter spoke, "Dad, I know I'm lucky."

"Luck has nothing to do with it, Peter."

"Yes, sir. What I meant to say is I have a chance to make something of myself, as you said, and I won't let Momma, you or Allen down."

Peter saw the trail of dust and knew the bus would be there in a few minutes. He and his dad climbed out of the truck and together pulled the two duffle bags from the back of the truck. The door of the bus opened. The driver climbed down the steps, then opened the baggage bin. Peter slung his duffle bags into the compartment and turned toward his dad. His father's outstretched hand signaled this was a man's way to leave.

Peter grasped his father's hand and said, "I'll write and I'll do my best."

*****

Peter boarded the bus and looked for a seat as the bus jerked into motion. A little boy had his head in his mother's lap. He could hear the child's soft snores. He passed an elderly couple speaking in low voices. He sat by a window near the back of the bus.

A middle-aged man in work clothes across the aisle from him asked, "Where are you going?"

"I've been given a scholarship to attend Blyne College."

The man commented, "It is a good school. You will earn a degree, but you will learn more by observing the people."

Peter pondered the man's words and wondered how his life would change. The blur of the woods changed to small farms, then houses close together. He put his head against the window and closed his eyes.

He slept until the bus driver said, "Blyne, last stop."

Peter stood and let the others off the bus before he bent his tall frame and climbed down the steps. The bus driver had all the luggage on the curb and had closed the bin when Peter retrieved his duffle bags. He looked up the street and down the street. He stood with a bag in each hand, unsure of the college location.

The man in work clothes who sat across the aisle from him on the bus called to Peter as he walked in the opposite direction, "Go around the square and take the road on the right. The college is about a quarter of a mile down that road. God bless you, son."

He waved as he turned and continued to walk away from Peter.

Peter looked around. The buildings were old. Some needed painting. Most were large two- and three-story houses with porches that wrapped around the side of them. A few were brick with stoops and awnings over the brightly painted front doors. Some had beautiful flower gardens and metal benches under towering trees for shade.

The last house on the left, a three-story wooden home, had been neglected. The paint had started to peel and the railing on the wraparound porch had spindles missing. The bushes needed trimming and the broken cement sidewalk needed repair. Peter wondered if this was the place he would work and live.

Across from the decaying house, he saw a large open field with short grass, trees with tall branches and others swooping to the ground. Adults were lying on quilts and the laughter of young children filled the air. He noticed an elderly couple walking hand in hand on the opposite side of this field, which he now realized was the city park.

So, this is Blyne. It looks like paradise to me, he said to himself. The white sign stood at the other end of this park. He ambled across the park, swinging his duffle bags. The sign indeed said Blyne College and underneath were arrows pointing to admissions, housing, Parker Hall, Gray's Library, and the cafeteria. He walked to the white wooden building with the sign Admissions Office above the door and went inside.

A gray-haired, elderly lady with wiry, curly hair, crow's feet at the corners of her eyes and spectacles on the edge of her nose, looked up and asked, "May I help you?"

"My name is Peter Cole and I have a letter stating I've been accepted at Blyne College. Is this where I find out what I am to do and where I will be living?"

The receptionist said, "The fall semester orientation is not until the last Monday in August. Why are you here so early? May I see the letter and any other paperwork you have received from the college?"

Peter took out the packet of information he had received. As he handed it to her, he said, "This is the letter saying I received a scholarship to attend college and this is the letter stating I will work with a maintenance man on painting and minor repairs from July 15th until classes start."

The receptionist said, "Let me see that letter."

She disappeared into another room and did not return for five minutes. When she did, she had a folder and began speaking as she approached the counter, "My supervisor told me you will be working with Mr. Bagwell. You are the first to arrive. Walk over to Yocum House and put your duffle bags down. Mr. Bagwell should be somewhere in the house.

"Yocum House is the last house on the south end of the town square. It is the three-story house that needs painting, lots of small repairs, and yard work. You should have seen it when you walked here.

"This office will schedule a tour of the school and show you where you will work tomorrow morning. Derek Hightower, an intern assigned to this office, will give you the tour. He will be a senior in the fall and is completing an internship this summer with this office. Expect him around eight in the morning."

Peter picked up his duffle bags and walked across the park. He paused by the huge Osage orange tree with its long thick arms reaching almost to the ground. He ducked his head and entered the tree's sheltered area. Peter took his lunch out of his duffle bag, then used the duffle bag as a pillow. He lay on the lush green grass and looked up at the umbrella of green branches that shaded him from the July heat. While lounging under the massive tree, he ate his two sandwiches and one sugar cookie his momma had made.

Peter saw a tall, muscular man in bibbed overalls come out of the gray house in need of repair. He jumped up, grabbed his duffle bags and ran over to introduce himself. Peter extended his hand and shook Mr. Bagwell's hand as he introduced himself. Mr. Bagwell said they would start work on the fifteenth when all four student workers had arrived.

Peter walked up the steps to the house. He went from room to room on the first floor with its squeaky, wooden floors. There were four very large rooms: kitchen, dining room, and two sitting rooms with sofas and leather armchairs. The walls were all the same shade of green. The kitchen wall had beads of grease above the gas stove.

Peter walked up the steps to the second floor. He found two identical bedrooms, each with four single beds and a small dresser in front of each. The rooms did not have curtains, so the sunlight filled the room. The bathroom at the end of the hall had a footed tub, a toilet, and a small square white sink on a steel frame. The door of the bedrooms had a listing of the four freshmen who would share each room. His name did not appear on either door on the second floor.

Peter went up to the third floor and found his name on one of the doors. He went in and tried sitting and bouncing on each mattress and decided on the one with the window behind it and a window to his right. He sat on the bed and bounced on it; as he lay on it, he didn't feel lumps in the mattress or the springs poking him in his back.

At eight o'clock the next morning, he heard someone with a deep, husky voice calling his name. He took the last spoonful of oatmeal and rinsed the bowl and spoon as his campus guide, Derek, came into the kitchen.

Derek explained he had been sent to give him a tour of the campus. Some of the buildings were two-story brick buildings and others gray frame buildings that looked like they had been built in the 1800s. All the buildings faced a quadrangle connected by cobblestone walkways. Wooden benches were scattered around the quadrangle.

They left the campus and walked downtown, turned a corner, then walked toward a split rail fence. Peter listened as Derek explained, "This farm is where you have been assigned to work. You will start the first week of September. There are two kinds of horses on this farm, work horses and race horses."

As Derek talked, Peter looked out at the lush, deep grass fields with horses grazing. On the far side of the field, he could see two white stables with steeples and dark green doors. They walked up a slight incline and rounded a bend before he saw the working farm. A red barn and two silos were near the white farmhouse. Fields of corn, hay, and tobacco surrounded it. They stopped and took in the view.

Derek said, "Mr. Cleburne owns this farm. You will work on the working farm caring for the work horses. He will schedule a time to meet with you before the semester starts. This is where I have worked for the past three years. As your letter stated, you will work twenty hours a week. The college and Mr. Cleburne set up your work schedule. I always had to start at 6:00 a.m. You are replacing me. I will work in the admissions office my senior year."

Peter's curiosity about the race horses had him inquire who worked with them and was responsible for their care. As they walked back to town, Derek told Peter those horses cost a lot of money and made a lot of money, if they won races. Mr. Cleburne had a staff that worked with those horses only.

They retraced their steps down the path and back to the park. Derek said goodbye and Peter decided to explore the town. The county courthouse with its dome and large clock seemed the focal point. Most of the shops were red brick or stone buildings. The sidewalks were cobblestone. Some of the bricks were pushed up, so he had to watch where he walked to keep from stumbling.

He passed a weaving shop with a bay window and stood there and watched a lady peddling the loom as her fingers guided the thread in place. Peter passed a metal shop with wide-open doors to let the heat from the welding fire escape. He stopped in front of a general merchandise store with clothes, shoes and craft items on display. He could see one person inside. A saddle shop dominated the corner. It smelled of leather and oils.

The whiff of food led him to turn the corner to see a large restaurant with large black words over the door. He paused and read, "Open for breakfast, lunch and supper, with the best home-cooked meals and desserts."

He wondered if students worked in all the shops. He was hungry just reading the sign. He continued his walk. Peter nodded as he passed the few students who were out in the middle of the day. He checked out the library, the cafeteria and one building he thought held classes, before returning to Yocum House. He spent the afternoon reading all the literature he received at the admissions office.

Before retiring, he got a postcard out of his duffle bag and wrote a note home:

"Dear Momma, Dad and Allen,

The college is not what I expected. We live in big houses, not dormitories, and we do all the work on the inside and the outside. I have been assigned to Yocum House, 42 Iota Street. I will share a room with three other fellows, but they haven't arrived yet. I will work on a farm twenty hours a week and care for work horses. The farm has race horses that live in white stables with tall steeples. There is a work side of the farm and a side for the race horses. I have been told I may begin my workday at six a.m. Tomorrow the other three students should arrive.

Love,

Peter"

Josephine (Jo) La Russa Graven

The Move

After Peter left for college, Flora, Tom and Allen finished the packing for the move. Lois came over for several days and helped Flora with the sorting and boxing of kitchen wares, linens and clothes.

On moving day, they were up early. Allen brought in the eggs as his mother made biscuits. They would need a hearty breakfast before loading the truck to make the long drive to the cabin. Lois helped Flora with the last of the kitchen packing as Tom, Billy Harold (Lois' husband), and Allen dismantled the beds and placed them on the truck, along with the wringer washer, flowery sofa, Tom's chair, the hutch, and a small table.

They turned the kitchen table upside down and filled it with boxes, the kitchen chairs, and a small wire pen for the chickens. Allen loaded a half cord of wood to further weigh down the table. The wood would be needed for cooking until they cut a few trees and cut them up for firewood. They tied down the bed of the truck with rope. Allen then spent a little time telling his friends goodbye.

Lois made sandwiches for them to eat on the way, filled a jar with water, and handed Flora two mason jars full of soup for their supper. Billy Harold gave Tom a box of shotgun shells as they stood by the truck and talked.

Billy Harold said, "I hate to see your family leave, but I understand. You have got to start over. At least you have a cabin that no one can take away from you."

He stretched out his hand as a gesture of friendship and a goodbye as Tom climbed in the truck. Lois and Flora both had tears in their eyes as they hugged and promised to keep in touch.

Tom waited a few minutes before motioning for his wife to climb in the truck. Allen got in after his mother. He hung his head out the window and watched as the home and the only life he'd known faded in the trail of dust.

They stopped at a roadside spot just inside Kentucky, climbed a slope full of wildflowers and ate the sandwiches Lois had made. Tom pulled a handful of fiery red flowers and handed them to his wife, then leaned over and gave her a kiss. The gesture made Flora smile. She had not experienced many smiles the past few months.

As they wound up the mountain, Flora's face clouded as she recalled the day her mother, her brother and she rode up this mountain, with their few possessions bouncing and rattling in the bed of her grandfather's truck with each pothole they hit. It seemed those same potholes were causing the household they had packed that morning to bounce and rattle, with the added squawking of the chickens. With each mile they traveled, she tightened her shoulders and wrenched her hands. She bit her lips in hopes of stopping the tears that were welling in the corners of her eyes.

Allen watched the land as they drove past thick forest, a few homes off in the distance, and none as nice as their home in Huntington had been. Smoke deep in the woods spiraled to the sky. He thought, *The smoke of bootleggers' stills. What would life be like in this bootlegger's haven? Would he have friends?* He always had plenty of things to do with his friends at home. It caught him off guard as he realized only the primitive cabin would be home. What about the school, would he have the same level of classes? Would the teachers challenge him? Would he be accepted? They dressed differently, spoke differently, and had experienced a much harder life than he had. He had two more years of school, then, with luck, maybe he could go somewhere else to work or go to college. Two years— such a long time.

No one spoke as they traveled the zigzagged road to the cabin. As Tom looked over at his wife and son, he could tell they were apprehensive about how their lives would change.

Tom had to concentrate on his driving, but kept looking off at the glint of guns shining through the trees near the road. He made a mental picture of the location of men in the woods and smoke from stills. He would avoid those areas. They were moving to a dangerous place, but not by choice.

He could kick himself for believing he'd always have a job operating the earth moving machinery for the coal company. If he hadn't spent above their means or if he'd gone elsewhere to look for a job, maybe they wouldn't be traveling this road to a primitive cabin in the middle of nowhere. He thought, *I don't even have a job and don't know how or where to look for work. Lord, please watch over us and give me direction for how to care for my family.*

Tom's hands tightened on the steering wheel when he saw the tops of trees on the drop-off side of the mountain and the narrow road hugging the mountain on the right. He knew he'd see the moss-covered planks in a few minutes. The wooden planks groaned as the truck rolled over them. The weeds and tall grass he'd cut on his first trip were as high as the side of the truck. The trees with kudzu hanging down from their branches made it appear they were traveling through a tunnel to reach the cabin.

Flora grabbed Tom's arm as he ran over a black snake. He laughed and asked her, "Would you like black snake steaks for supper?"

It broke the silence and tension, and all three laughed.

Tom pulled the truck as close as he could to the cabin door. Allen opened the truck door, but looked to make sure no snake slithered across the yard.

Flora went into the house and called to Allen, "Bring in a few pieces of firewood. It may be summer, but there is a damp feeling inside here."

Allen snickered when he came in with an armload of wood. His momma had the broom they had left on their first visit in her hand and stared at the floor for four-legged creatures or snakes slithering across the floor.

She saw him snickering and said, "I'm just checking, Allen. Now you stop laughing at me."

Both Tom and Allen were in a fit of laughter when Flora put her head out the door and said, "I heard that."

The laughter was contagious, and Flora was laughing as hard as they were. Tom said, "Woman, come give your man a kiss."

Flora and Allen took the squawking chickens into the house and closed them up on the screened-in back porch. Tom and his son took the wire fence off the truck.

Tom got his hammer and went around to the side of the house and called to his son, "Get the hoe and dig holes for the posts. I'll tack the wire and we will have a temporary coop put up. I don't want your mother cooking one of those chickens our first night here, but fried chicken would be a tasty supper."

It took several hours to get the eight posts deep enough to support the fence. Allen strung the fence and his dad nailed it to each post.

Flora looked at her surroundings and wondered how they were going to make it here. It had been an unhappy place for her as a child. The inside of the cabin reminded her of their first house, the duplex with the squeaky floors, bare windows and light bulbs hanging from black cords in the ceiling.

Flora smiled as she thought about the newer furniture they had purchased since they married. She looked at all the windows and knew she could alter the curtains from her old home. She could make it look like a home. It would take time. She said to herself, *Life is just what it is, so accept it, Flora.*

It took the rest of the afternoon to unload the truck. Tom teased Flora about those squawking critters on the back porch before he took them to the temporary coop. She swatted him with the wet cloth she had in her hand as he ran out the door laughing. Laughter had been absent from their home for a long time. It felt good to hear it.

Father and son worked on putting the beds together, and Flora looked through the boxes for the bed linens as she directed the placement of furniture unloaded and brought inside.

She said, "Tom, put the hutch against the wall. No, no, not that wall, the living room wall that goes into the kitchen. That's it."

Flora continued to give orders to her son of what she wanted unloaded next. She stuck her head out the door and yelled, "Allen, bring in the box marked dishes, and don't drop them. Those are the dishes your grandmother Cole gave your dad and me when we married."

Flora looked outside to check on what needed to come into the house before dark.

"Put the washer on the porch near the kitchen window, in front of the sink. The hose will need to connect to the faucet on wash day."

Allen climbed up on the bed of the truck to help his dad with the washer. Tom realized he'd need Allen on the ground to help get the washer down and called to his wife, "Honey, I need you to help get the washer off the truck. I need Allen down here and you in the truck bed to push the washer to the edge."

He lifted his wife onto the truck bed and Tom and Allen stood at the edge to catch the washer as Flora rolled it forward. It took all their strength to hold onto the round tub and bring it down. Tom said, "Easy does it. Now, let's set it on the ground and let me get your momma down."

At dusk the last of the furniture and all the boxes were unloaded. All boxes had labels and her men put them in the rooms where they would be unpacked.

Flora got a set of clothes for each of them for the next day, then went into the kitchen to warm the soup Lois had given them, while her husband took his pocketknife and cut cardboard to cover the broken windows.

They sat down at the table and Tom reached for their hands as they bowed their heads for the blessing.

Tom said, "Dear Lord, bless this food our neighbor has shared. We are thankful for this bounty and, dear Lord, guide us in our beginnings here in this cabin. Amen."

Tom squeezed his wife and son's hand before releasing them. Flora ate one bowl of soup as her hungry men finished their first bowl then drained the pot of the remaining soup. Flora seemed tense and had a faraway look as she held her spoon in mid-air.

Her husband asked her, "What are you thinking? You seem deep in thought."

Her husband and son waited for her to speak. A tear trickled down her cheek.

After another tear rolled down her cheek, she said, "My thoughts. I thought about my life here as a child. I wonder how we will be accepted by the people who live on this mountain. We are different. We are city folks. We have had so much more than these people. Can we fit in?"

He put his hand over her hand, gave it a squeeze and said, "It will take time. The people here will realize over time that we are a family trying to exist, just as they are."

Tom told his son, "You will find it more difficult than your mother or me. Everything and every person here is new to you. You have always lived in the same place and had the same set of friends. Your mother and I have lived in different places and learned to adjust to the changes."

Allen remarked, "I saw the smoke of stills and the glint of guns in the woods as we came up the mountain. How safe are we? Can we fit in?"

His dad replied, "We have no choice, son."

The packing, loading and unloading had them exhausted. After supper, Tom and Allen went on the porch and talked about what they needed to do the next day, while Flora cleaned the kitchen. Tom's mind wouldn't stop. There were so many tasks that needed to be done as soon as possible.

"First thing in the morning, we need to clear enough of the area around the cabin to prevent wildlife from coming up to the cabin. We also need to dig a garden bed. Your momma can plant the seeds we brought. We will need the crops to eat when harvested and for your mother to can for winter."

Flora came outside, drying her hands and asked, "What is it that you want me to do?"

Tom looked up and commented, "Plant a garden, but tonight we need to get a good night's sleep. It has been a long day."

The Storm

The first few weeks at the cabin, Tom and Allen worked all day digging a garden spot for Flora. Tom had sold the property he had inherited after his mother's death and sold her old tractor to a neighboring farmer. A few years later, Tom bought a newer tractor from a Sears & Roebuck catalog. He'd only had it four years when he lost his job and had to sell it. A pickaxe, shovel, and hoe had replaced the tractor.

Sweat poured down their faces and soaked their shirts as the sun scorched both them and the hard dry ground. It hadn't rained in the three weeks they had lived on the mountain, so Tom hoped a good soaking rain would come soon. They piled the brush away from the cabin and pulled the menacing poison sumac from the edge of the plank path in the morning. After lunch Tom planned to show his son how to fell a tree.

Allen had never cut down a tree. He'd only chopped the logs into firewood. Today, he'd learn how to safely cut down a tree. His dad got the axe and wedge from the shed at the back of the cabin. He took his son to a wooded area near the property line.

He said, "Son, there are several things you need to remember when you cut down a tree in a dense area. First, look at the size of the tree and what is around it. Always have someone with you. Accidents do happen."

Allen listened as they walked through a thicket.

His dad asked, "Do you see that pine tree that is leaning toward that big elm?"

Allen replied, "Yes, sir."

"If you tried to cut the pine tree, it would get hung up in the elm tree. You'd be in danger of it getting wedged between the elm tree and the pine's trunk. Look around. What tree do you believe would be safe to cut down?"

Allen walked for a few minutes. He looked at the size of trees. He looked at the distance from other trees and other trees' sizes that might interfere with it falling clear.

He said, "Dad, this tree," as he pointed at a twenty-foot hickory tree, "isn't so tall it would hang on another tree coming down. Its trunk is about eighteen inches in diameter. It is a hickory tree, so it would be good firewood when it dries out. "

Tom was amazed. His son was so serious, so observant, and so methodical in his thinking. He gave his son a pat on his back and a big smile.

"You made a good choice. Now you need to learn how to cut it down. Get the axe and the steel wedge. Place the wedge about eighteen inches above the base of the tree. The wedge should be driven into the side you expect the tree to fall, then remove it. The cut allows the tree to slowly fall as you drive the steel wedge deeper on the other side. The steel will slice through the trunk."

His dad took the axe and steel wedge, tapped the wedge at an angle, then put the axe over his shoulder and brought it down with all his strength. The sound of the axe against the tree echoed through the mountain. His dad handed him the axe and wedge and said, "Now it is your turn."

Allen was nervous. He'd split logs before but had never felled a tree. Chips of wood whizzed past him. It felt good to whack that tree. Sweat beaded on his forehead and ran down his face.

"Now, son," his father said, "You have chipped enough on that side. On this side, you want to chip out enough so the wedge is about six inches higher and is driven in at an angle. In between each blow, wiggle the axe blade to get it out."

Allen felt a sense of exhilaration at hearing the sound of the first tree he felled. They worked all day and stopped for water every hour. Saplings were cut to thin the wooded area, then split for firewood.

*****

Flora could hear the crack of the axe against the trees as she hoed her garden. Deep furrows lay behind her. Strands of wet hair fell into her face as she dropped seeds in the hills and covered them with dirt. She straightened up and arched her back to relieve the aching muscles.

She scooped a dipper of spring water and brought it to her parched lips. It was warm as it slid down her throat. She dipped into the bucket of water a second time and slowly poured it over her head. Sweat, mingled with warm water, trickled through her hair and across her blistered face as it continued downward across the swell of her breast, into the pockets of her apron, then squeezing through the fabric on its journey to her legs and to the dirt.

Flora looked up at the fast-moving clouds that covered the sun. They were rain clouds. She hurriedly dropped seeds in the hills and covered the mounds with dirt. She planted row after row. The wind picked up. The sky darkened, large drops of rain cooled her as she first walked, then ran for the cabin.

As the wind intensified, Flora tried to run, but met resistance. Her skirt billowed out then snapped at her legs. She put her back to the side wall of the cabin and inched her way to the steps and the door. She looked to see if Tom and Allen were in sight, but saw nothing but sheets of rain sweeping across the land. She forced the door open and was knocked down as it slammed behind her.

*****

Tom and Allen had seen the gathering storm, but wanted to finish cutting the young sapling. Tom kept looking at the changing sky—gray, black, then green. The wind was howling, and pine trees were bending as raindrops spattered the ground. Animals scurried for shelter. With the last blow of the axe, the tree fell between the tall pines before crashing to the ground. The chorus of birds ceased.

In the distance came the sound of a freight train. The swirling debris and the black funnel were bearing down on them. Tree limbs cracked. Trees snapped and fell.

Tom grabbed his son, threw him to the ground, and belly-walked between the two felled trees to lie on top of him as the blackness overshadowed them and torrents of rain soaked them. His father said, "It will be alright. Just pray."

Allen, in a state of panic, cried out, "But Momma!"

"It is too late. The storm is here. Your mother would have seen it coming. She is alright," his dad reassured him.

The wind roared as the weight of the pine trees trapped them underneath. Then there was silence. Light began to filter through the branches, so Tom knew the storm had passed. He tested the space he had. They had little head room.

Tom said, "Allen, inch your way out between the two trees."

Tom lifted his muddy body and his son began to belly-crawl toward the light. They slid their bodies through the mud and over the pebbles, small branches and wood chips, until free. Trees were down all around them. Allen ran, stumbled, and ran again through the rain to reach his momma.

He yelled, "Momma, Momma, Momma!"

He heard nothing and saw a flattened path with trees scattered like toothpicks. The two stately elms that stood on either side of the cabin crisscrossed the front of the cabin and blocked it from view. They climbed over fallen trunks and pushed their way through the wall of limbs until they could see the cabin was still standing. Strips of tin roof lay on the ground. Curls of roofing were still attached. Tattered curtains hung from the broken window.

Panic overcame Tom as he raced for the door. They reached the porch about the same time and could hear Flora praying and crying. Tom pushed open the door as Allen crashed into him. They found her covered in grit, rocking back and forth under the table. Tom knelt down and crawled under the table. He cradled his wife until her tensed body relaxed, her cries changed to an occasional gasp, and her trembling stopped.

Tom tried to reassure her, "It's alright. The storm has passed. We aren't hurt. It's alright."

Allen clung to his parents with fear still in his eyes. Rain poured through the opening in the roof like a waterfall. They stayed under the table until the rain stopped and the sky cleared.

Opportunity Came Calling

Light flooded the room. There was a peacefulness in the wee hours of morning. It was the time of day Tom savored. He turned his head and felt the tickle of Flora's hair against his face. She had slept in his arms with her body pressed against his. She had her arm across his chest and her fingers on his shoulder. He turned enough to kiss her fingers, then her hair, and listened to her soft breaths. He closed his eyes and drifted back to sleep.

A short time later, he heard his son's soft steps as he went out to the chicken coop to retrieve eggs for breakfast. Tom slipped his arm out from under Flora and climbed out of bed. He pulled on his pants and went in the kitchen as Allen came in with the eggs.

He remarked, "The hens didn't lay many eggs. I guess the storm scared them, too."

His dad nodded, "Speak quietly. Let your mother sleep. She had a very frightening day."

He spooned coffee into the coffee pot and put it on to brew. His wife came into the kitchen as she tied the belt of her bathrobe.

Tom took his wife in his arms and gave her a kiss. He winked at her and said with a chuckle in his voice, "Woman, if your kisses get any better, I don't know if I'll be able to contain myself. Allen will have to do all the cleaning up while I chase you around the house."

Flora smiled that knowing smile and pushed her husband aside. Allen grinned at his parents' playfulness as he cracked the eggs.

After breakfast, Tom emptied the pots of rainwater that lay around the house from yesterday's storm. It would take weeks to clear the path to the road. The downed trees assured him they would have plenty of wood for winter.

Before going outside, he wrapped the Ace bandage tightly around his foot damaged in the railroad accident long ago, then put on his work boots. He walked down the steps, breaking off some branches and pushing others off the house. He pulled limbs off the truck to see deep scratches, but no real damage.

As he retraced his steps to the porch, his son came outside and asked, "Dad, your truck?"

Tom brushed off the wet leaves from his clothing as he spoke, "Only scratches to the truck. Allen, we need to clear away the limbs close to the cabin first, so we can repair the roof. Over the next few weeks, we will work on clearing the path to the road. Get the axe off the back porch and help me clear enough to get on the roof."

Tom walked around to the small tool shed and took out the ladder that he had found inside. He leaned it against the side of the house, then went around to the front of the cabin, picked up his work gloves and called, "Flora, come out here and hold the base of the ladder while I climb up and check the damage."

Allen had chopped away the limbs closest to the cabin by the time his dad leaned the ladder against the house. Allen dragged them off the cabin and away from it. Flora pushed against the ladder to keep it from moving, as Tom climbed halfway up, turned, and saw the twisted piece of tin roof in the field near the woodshed. The twisted piece of tin could be hammered to straighten it.

He climbed the rest of the way up the ladder and saw the curled metal strip partly clinging to the roof by a couple of nails. It would be harder to straighten them from their attached points. He looked at it for a long time, then decided he could use a flat piece of tree limb to hold the tin down. He could drive nails into the tin, and move the flat limb a little further until the exposed section was covered. He would need his son's help with the roof.

Tom and Allen laid the twisted sheet of the roof on the ground and began hammering. By lunch time they had the piece flattened and on the roof. Tom looked at the fallen trees for a branch he could cut. He chose a branch six inches in diameter, cut it, then sliced one side flat. The afternoon sun began shifting as he mounted the roof with a pocket full of nails and the flat limb.

All afternoon he slid the board a little farther until he had that sheet of tin in place. At dusk he laid the ladder on the front porch and went in to clean up for supper. His clothes were soaked with perspiration. His hair, dripping of sweat, was matted to his head.

Flora and Allen spent the afternoon clearing away limbs near the cabin. Allen cut the limbs and his momma stacked the small limbs she'd cleared of leaves near the house. She raked the leaves to a cleared area ready for burning.

When Tom stopped for the day, Flora and Allen put their tools on the porch and went inside. They were as drenched as Tom. Allen got a towel and went to the spring water pond and dove in. Flora turned on the kitchen faucet, put her head under the stream of water, and let the sweat swirl down the drain. She ran her arms through the water then dried her face and arms with the dish towel. She put on a clean apron and got down her mixing bowl.

She made a pan of cornbread, opened a jar of last summer's black-eyed peas and a jar of turnips, then put them on the stove to warm. While the cornbread baked, she washed the blackberries she'd picked from the bramble bushes the morning of the storm. She took her big skillet off the back of the stove and poured the washed berries in it. Even though she was very tired, she was happy. She hummed "This Old Place Of Mine" as she added water, flour, and sugar to the berries.

Tom and Allen smiled when they saw the meal. They were starved. They ate every morsel. Allen even took a spoon and scraped every drop of berry juice from the skillet. Her husband and son were sound asleep in the living room and snoring loudly by the time she finished the dishes. She shook them and sent them to bed and she followed.

For the rest of the week, they spent their days clearing limbs and stacking them on the side of the house. Flora continued to remove small branches and twigs and pile them in the clearing away from the side of the cabin. Every night Tom burned the leaves she raked. As the moonlight cast shadows, they sat on the porch steps.

Saturday morning, as they worked in the yard, they heard someone with a deep, husky voice greet them. "Hello! You folks okay?"

A heavy-set, gray-haired, older fellow with a potbelly, and two tall, thin lumberjacks appeared out of the maze of downed trees.

"That storm took down half the trees in the area," the older man said, as he reached out his hand to Tom. "My name is Michael McCord and these two are my sons, Jeb and Ted. We live down the road a bit. I own the timber business around these parts."

"My name is Tom Cole. This is my wife, Flora, and our younger son, Allen."

Mr. McCord looked around, "If he is your younger son, where is your older son?"

"He starts college in September at Blyne College. He is working at the college this month as part of his scholarship."

"He must be a smart kid to get a scholarship to go to college. Well, that isn't what I came to talk about. A lot of trees are down. I need help stripping them and loading them. I have to clear the ones blocking the road first, then clear the trees that were blown down in the woods. It is a twelve-hour day, six days a week. I will pay you, Mr. Cole, $10 a day; and, son, I will pay you $6 a day. Are you willing to work?"

Tom didn't hesitate. He nodded his head and extended his hand to Mr. McCord. McCord took his hand and gave it a vigorous shake.

"Good. Be at the road Monday morning at 6 a.m. with food and water for the day."

He turned to Flora. "Mrs. Cole, don't burn those twigs. My wife uses them to make wreaths and baskets. I'll ask her to come over. You churchgoing folks? There is a little white church about a mile down the road. On the last Sunday of the month, there is a picnic lunch on the church grounds after the service. It would be a good time to meet the folks who live on this mountain. You have a good day." He tipped his ball cap and turned to leave, with his two silent sons behind him.

After Mr. McCord and his sons disappeared in the forest of downed trees, Flora sucked in her breath and said, "WOW! Tom, did you hear what he said? He'll pay you $10 a day and pay Allen $6 a day. That is more money than you were making with the coal company. My momma used to say, when God takes away something in one hand, He always provides something better."

Tom picked up his wife and whirled her around. "Yes, baby, I did."

Allen was calculating in his head how many days were left before school started and how much he would earn if he could work most of them. He took an empty coffee can his mother kept on the back porch to his room to fill with his earnings.

They worked the rest of that day clearing the yard. Tom and Allen used the two-man saw to cut the large branches, while Flora sawed the smaller branches into pieces of firewood. Large pieces were set aside for splitting, when they had time.

*****

Tom and Allen had worked for Mr. McCord for a couple of weeks, when he told them he would pay them $25 for each stripped tree with a girth of at least thirty inches.

McCord said, "It will take another week or two to clear the roads and deliver the logs to the sawmill."

Tom told his wife, "We can work in our spare time clearing our trees."

Flora raised her voice in reply, "Spare time! What spare time, when you work from six in the morning until six or seven at night, six days a week?"

"Baby, it doesn't get dark in the summertime in these hills until nine o'clock. I'd have an hour each night to do a little. I know Sunday is the Lord's day, but I think He'd understand if I worked on my own place after church. It's just for a little while."

*****

Allen collected the eggs each morning as his momma started breakfast. He filled the gallon jug with water and set it by the door. Tom made the lunch sandwiches and Flora added a slice of pound cake to each. Allen and Tom wolfed down breakfast. Tom gave his wife a kiss on the top of her head and Allen gave her a hug on the porch before racing to the road.

Flora cleaned the kitchen and made the beds, then dressed in her flour sack dress and put on her apron with deep pockets. She shooed the chickens out of the coop and collected the droppings, then she used her apron to guide the chickens back into the coop. She spent the rest of the morning pulling weeds in her garden and sprinkling the droppings between the rows of her garden.

Blooms of yellow were everywhere. Flora would have plenty of vegetables for canning. She got her big wash tub and returned to the garden.

She picked beans, field peas, tomatoes, squash, zucchini and cucumbers. She pulled back the husk and silks and pressed the sweet juice from the corn. It needed a few more days on the stalk. The plump tomatoes were put in the deep pockets of her apron. Her arm muscles were taut as she struggled to reach the porch with the overflowing tub of vegetables. She rinsed the vegetables and laid them on a towel in the kitchen to dry. She poured the rinse water over her herb garden beside the house.

It was Tuesday, laundry day. Flora collected the sheets, towels and dirty clothes and brought them to the porch. She pulled the wringer washer to the window and put the hose inside the kitchen window to hook the hose to the faucet. As the machine agitated, she put the field peas in a pot and took them outside to shell. She hung the wet laundry on the three clothes lines Tom had strung, returned to the porch, and was shelling peas when she heard someone call her name.

A tall, aged lady fanning herself with one hand and holding a pie in the other, approached.

"Are you Flora, Flora Cole? I'm Emmy McCord. My husband told me about you. I thought I'd come introduce myself. I don't get to visit much with so much gardening and housework. You know what that is like."

"Yes, I'm Flora. Join me on the porch where it is cooler. Can I get you a glass of water?"

Emmy offered to help shell peas and Flora brought out another pot. As they shelled, Emmy told Flora about making and selling baskets and wreaths for the October Days Celebration in Blyne. Emmy said, "There must be two thousand city folks there. Have you ever been?"

"No, we haven't. Our son Peter is attending Blyne College. He won't get home until Christmas break."

Emmy asked, "What is he studying?"

"He's studying forestry."

Emmy continued, "If you can go in October, you will see all the crafts and furniture they sell."

Flora asked, "What kind of crafts are for sale?"

"Pottery, leather goods, weavings, paintings, wood furniture, baskets, wreaths, jam, jelly, pickles, homemade candy, and quilts. There is always a band playing in the park and families having picnics by the river," Emmy said.

They had shelled for an hour before Emmy asked Flora about attending church.

"Did you go to church before moving here? Michael said he mentioned to you and your husband that there is a small church about a mile away. Sunday service is at ten o'clock and the last Sunday of the month the congregation share a meal after the service. This coming Sunday will be the last Sunday in August."

Flora started to reply when they heard the first rumble of thunder and both women looked up with apprehension. Emmy put the shelled pea pot down and stood. "I'd best get home. I don't want to get caught in a thunderstorm."

She hurried down the plank path as Flora grabbed her wash tub to gather her lines of laundry.

*****

Torrents of rain pelted the men as they heaved the last log onto the logging truck and secured the chains. McCord paid the men and sent them home. Mudslides and washes the rain was creating made it too dangerous for logging.

Tom sent Allen home and he walked into town. He stopped at the hardware store to have glass panes cut. He walked across the street to the mercantile store and purchased a piece of floral print for Flora. She could make new curtains for the kitchen and maybe a tablecloth for the kitchen table. He added three sticks of butterscotch candy as the clerk rang up his purchases.

Josephine (Jo) La Russa Graven

Icy Greeting

Sunday morning, Flora put on her green dress and black heels she had ordered from Sears & Roebuck. She took the curlers out of her hair, brushed it, and put on her white straw hat with the green and yellow ribbons and bow. Both of the McCords had mentioned a picnic after church service. She had packed the picnic basket with food, plates, silverware and a tablecloth by the time Tom and Allen had dressed for church. Their shoes were polished. Their slacks pressed with creases. Their oxford cloth shirts and ties finished their Sunday attire.

The parking area at the church had few cars when they arrived. Flora judged from the near-empty parking area that few attended church. They saw no one walking or driving to the church. They looked around as they walked up the three steps to the church and Tom opened the door.

Every pew had families. Tom nodded to those who stared at them as they went down the aisle. Every time they stopped at a pew, those seated spread out and left no room for them. This happened at each row. They turned and walked to the back of the church and stood throughout the service.

As the minister concluded with the blessing and announced to set up the food tables, Tom, Flora and Allen left the church and went back to their truck. Flora and Allen had already climbed into the truck, ready to leave, when Mr. McCord came running over to them. He took Tom's arm and said, "Don't leave. If you didn't bring food, you can share ours. Emmy always makes extra."

Then he noticed the nice picnic basket in the truck bed. Mr. McCord continued talking, "Tom, several of the men work for me. You work with them every day. Mrs. Cole, Emmy will introduce you to the ladies; and Allen, the young folks always have their own table. You will fit right in."

Reluctantly, they climbed out of the truck and followed Mr. McCord to the picnic tables. They saw the aged wooden table filled with food. Flora knew she would not take her embroidered tablecloth out of her basket. Plates of fried squirrel and stewed rabbit filled the table. Jars of green beans and tomatoes added color to the table. Berry pies were hidden under towels to keep the flies and bees out of them.

Flora set out the bowl of fried chicken, the loaf of homemade bread, fried potatoes, and pickled squash. She put the plate of sugar cookies she'd made with the desserts.

The women watched as she added the food from her basket. No one spoke. Plain white plates and metal plates sat in front of the locals. It embarrassed Flora to bring out her beautiful flowered plates her mother-in-law had given them when they had married. At that moment, she realized how much more they had than these hard-working mountain people.

Emmy realized the tension and spoke up. "Ladies, this is Flora Cole. She lived here for a few years as a child. She is Ester and Ezekiel Tully's granddaughter. They have moved into her grandparents' cabin. Her husband, Tom, works for my husband as a lumberjack. Don't be standoffish. Her momma grew up in these mountains. Introduce yourselves."

As they passed the food, the women said their names and gave a faint smile. Flora repeated each name and said, "I'm glad to meet you."

Allen sat with the older boys, who left him only an edge of the bench. All were taller and more muscular than he. All had on worn jeans and scuffed boots. Their hair didn't look like it had been combed. With plates piled high with food, they joked back and forth, but ignored Allen. As Allen sat silent and observed them, he wondered, *What's my life going to be like here? How will I have to change to fit in?*

Tom and the mountain men talked. They were curious as to why a city fellow wanted to live in that old abandoned cabin. Tom explained losing his job and then losing the house. They had something in common. Both had faced and were facing hard times. Several of the bootleggers didn't believe his story and thought he might be a government agent planted there to spy on their stills.

They would not let him near their stills and would keep their guns close by if they saw him snooping around.

On the way home, the family talked about the icy greeting they had encountered at the church. Flora said, "We have all the nice clothes and Sunday shoes. They wear worn work clothes to church. We are the city outsiders invading their space and they want to know why."

Allen sat in the truck with a feeling of uncertainty about his life in this place. He knew one thing for certain. He wouldn't wear dress clothes and dress shoes next Sunday to church.

Tom felt working with some of these men clearing the trees downed by the storm would ease their mistrust of him. Sharing the meal at the church picnic jolted him to the reality of living in Appalachia. He realized how much his family had before the layoff and how little these people had, yet they were happy.

Shared Lives

The heat of the August sun bore down on Flora as she pulled the last of her squash, beans, peas, okra, tomatoes and corn. The plants were almost dead and wilted leaves fell to the ground. Soon she would pull up the dead stalks and prepare the soil for the winter garden. The garden took up one quarter of the yard. She had plenty of work canning, and she was happy knowing the uncertainty of how long Mr. McCord would need Tom to clear the trees.

Flora bought an old, battered, somewhat rusty, child's wagon at the hardware store's backyard junk pile for a dollar. She used it for pulling the wash tub to the clothesline rather than lifting the heavy tub of laundry as she had been doing. She used it to collect vegetables from her garden, weeds, and underbrush near the cabin.

Tom had built shelving in two corners of the kitchen, and built more higher up all around the kitchen. The larger garden produced so much that all the shelves were full. The cabin did not have a root cellar, so she'd have to store her winter vegetables on the back porch.

Flora set aside food for supper, went out on the porch and shucked corn, then shelled peas. She soaked some of the peas for supper. She would put the rest in a three-gallon bucket with a lid for winter after they had dried. She canned all she'd picked that day and stored it on the back porch with a cloth over it.

By noon she had her canning done for the day. Flora walked through the path Tom and Allen had cleared connecting the Coles' house and the McCords' property. Tom and Allen used the path to meet Mr. McCord each morning for work. Flora and Emmy used it often to visit. There were still plump blackberries along that path and Flora took a shiny bucket with her to fill. They'd make a good cobbler to finish off supper.

When Emmy first visited Flora, she told her about weaving baskets and making wreaths to sell. Emmy gathered tender vines and long grasses of different colors from the Coles' rubbish pile, and twigs that had been put on the side of the house after the storm. Emmy promised to show Flora how to weave and make baskets once she finished her summer canning.

On Thursday, Emmy had a bucket of twigs pliable enough to create the base of a basket. She invited Flora to her house and showed Flora how to intertwine the twigs to make the base. Emmy pulled out some twigs from the water bucket and told Flora to pull out some about the same size. She laid down seven twigs with a small space between each twig. Flora did the same. Emmy took out another twig from the water bucket and began to weave it between the twigs. She did this with six more twigs.

Flora watched, then tried to duplicate Emmy's movements. Emmy pulled out another twig and bent it to start the sides of the basket. Flora clumsily tried to weave the side twig. Emmy helped her, then decided they would need to soak more twigs before they could continue.

They sat on the porch, sipped cool tea, and fanned themselves as they shared their lives.

Emmy said, "I was raised in these mountains. My family had more than most families. We had a wooden house my granddaddy built. We all lived together. I had a brother and a sister, but both died of whooping cough before I was born. Momma and Grandma did all the work around the house and the land. Daddy and Granddaddy worked for the state putting up lines for electricity. We used kerosene lamps until 1928. I got married that year to Luther Riley and another room was added to the house for us.

"We had two boys, age eleven and twelve, when Luther and Daddy went to the war. Life was hard for us for a few years until the men returned after the war. By then, Granddaddy was down with lumbago. Grandma would rub him down every morning with the root salve she made. It would help for a few hours, then he had to go back to bed for the rest of the day. Grandma did what she could, and my mother and I cared for the land.

"A soldier named Michael McCord was in my daddy's unit and said he wanted to meet the family, if they lived through the war.

"My first husband, Luther, a marine, died in the Battle of the Point, Bataan, on Friday, February 13, 1942. It was difficult for my boys and me to accept.

"Daddy brought Michael home with him after the war ended. It was cramped in the house, but we made do. We were married June 1, 1946. Michael was sent from God, I know. He's been the best husband and wonderful father to my boys. He helped Daddy string line for a while, then they began cutting timber and floating it down the river to the lumber yard.

"I've rambled on about myself. Tell me about your family. You and your brother were just children when your momma moved back after your daddy died."

Flora looked down and knotted her hands before she looked at Emmy and began to share. "I was told my mother went to visit my Aunt Eula May in Harlow, Kentucky, when she was fifteen. She got a job at Woolworth's soda fountain. My dad came in every day after work and got a sandwich and a piece of pie. They talked every day, fell in love, and married when she was sixteen and he was seventeen.

"I don't remember much about my childhood in Harlow, Kentucky, other than it was a small coal mining community. We lived in company housing with electricity and an indoor toilet. Everything seemed to have a black film of coal dust. Between the coal mines and strip mines, it is a wonder everybody didn't have black lung. It was depressing, but I didn't realize it at that time.

"After Daddy died in a mining accident, we had to vacate the company housing within a month. Momma wrote home and her daddy came after us. We lived with my grandparents on this mountain for a few years before

Momma got a job filling out forms for a coal mining company in Ashland, Kentucky.

"I met Tom at church and a year later we were married. He worked for the railroad until the accident with the railroad tie that fell on his foot, crushing some bones in the foot, and breaking his leg. We had to move in with his mother because the foot didn't heal and he couldn't find a job.

"I went to work at a bread factory until he got a job operating one of those earth moving machines for the coal company in a nearby town over the state line in West Virginia. Tom commuted the twelve miles each day while we continued to live with his mother.

"He saved money weekly and we eventually bought an abandoned house from the bank. He worked on repairs on Sundays for half a year before we could move into our own home. His mother was kicked by her mule and died not long after that. Tom sold her property to a neighbor farmer and we had money to buy things for our home.

"Like you and Luther, we had our two boys close together. Tom built a fence around the yard. He wanted it to be a safe place for the boys to play. I stayed home, tended my garden, and raised a few chickens. Tom operated one of those big earth moving machines. His job paid enough to pay for the house and buy a new truck the year before the layoff.

"After the layoff, he couldn't find a permanent position—so many men had been laid off. He stood on the corner every morning in hopes of work as a day laborer.

It didn't pay much, but it helped pay some of the bills. He traded his truck at the dealership for the twenty-year-old truck he now drives. It helped some, but we couldn't pay the house note, and after six months the bank was going to foreclose; but the bank gave us a three-month extension on it. We sold everything that we could to survive. I was cleaning out the china cabinet when I found the family album.

"I had looked through it and left it on the table. A friend dropped by with a string of fish her husband had caught that morning. She saw the picture album and opened it. She saw the picture of the cabin and asked about it. I had put it out of my mind. I had never mentioned to Tom that it might still be standing and that I inherited it when Momma died, then my brother died in a mine explosion.

"My friend, Lois, made a comment before she left that day that God had a plan. He was just testing our faith. I thought about that the rest of the day. I shared the picture of the cabin with Tom and told him that, if it hadn't been devoured by kudzu, it belonged to us. He went to the Grayson County Courthouse, found the property records, drove up here and now we are here."

Emmy asked about her oldest son. "Your son, Peter, is in college at Blyne?"

Flora replied, "Yes, that must have been part of God's plan. Just before Peter graduated from high school, his school counselor talked to him about college at Blyne and did the paperwork. They gave him an academic scholarship. Someone in the admissions office asked if he wanted to come mid-July and help spruce up the student housing being added where he'd be living. He'd live there, have meals and receive $75 pay for the six weeks of work. His classes started a few weeks ago. I miss him so."

Emmy told Flora, "When you visit him, you will see all the handcrafted baskets, wreaths, and, pottery."

Josephine (Jo) La Russa Graven

Weaving Baskets and Friendship

It was about noon on a Monday when Flora walked through the path between her cabin and Emmy's home. Emmy put down her needlework when she saw her neighbor and asked, "You finish your canning for the day? What did you put up?"

Flora waved and replied, "I made soup base with the last of the vegetables. Hot soup will taste good on cold winter days. The garden is dried up. In a week or two, I'll start my winter garden, but I want to know more about weaving a basket first."

Flora had a lard can full of wild strawberries and blackberries she found along the path. The bright red strawberries and the big plump blackberries almost looked like a Christmas present in the silvery can. They'd make a good cobbler for supper and there should be enough for another jar or two of jam.

Emmy called to her, "Looks like the blackberries are still plentiful. Where did you find them? I'll get me some tomorrow, if there are any left."

"Emmy, there are enough for you and me to pick again as well as all the bees in that thicket, but watch that big cluster of bushes by the small elm tree. Those are the biggest berries you have ever seen on those plants, but the closer you get the louder the rattlers. It is full of rattlesnakes."

"Don't tell my husband or he will be out there killing those snakes and we will be eating them for supper. Have you ever eaten rattlesnake? It tastes like chicken, only tougher."

Flora shivered at the thought of eating snake and said, "I'm not that hard up for meat that I want to eat rattlesnake."

Emmy and Flora had the flat weaving of the basket base completed. Today, Emmy showed Flora how to create the circle of weaving to make the sides. Emmy pulled a dark green piece of grass and held it around the base frame to see if it was long enough. Flora's eyes were glued to Emmy's movements as she listened to Emmy's explanation of why she measured the length of grass against the basket frame. Flora picked up a dark green piece of grass and tried to duplicate the measuring in her own weaving.

Emmy said, "Flora, we will create a pattern by changing the color and the coarseness of grasses we weave."

Flora watched as Emmy wove the two rows of dark green grass, then seven rows of a narrow light green grass before repeating the pattern. Flora struggled to get the first piece between the twig framing. Emmy watched, but said nothing as Flora worked the grass in place. More grass would have to be cut before they could finish the baskets.

Flora hoped she would have one or two to take to Blyne for the big October celebration and for the Madison County fair competition in Blyne. She had never entered anything in the fair. She had put aside several jars of jam and pickles to enter. Emmy had told her they gave ribbons for the best in categories of jelly, jam, pickles, fruit and vegetables.

The sunlight shifted and Emmy put the baskets on the mantle. Emmy picked up a bowl and handed it to Flora to examine, and said, "I made it."

Flora looked at the earthen bowl with its coiled sides and rich red color. Emmy handed her another bowl and said, "I made it, too. I am getting better. I added berry juice to the clay to get the red color."

Emmy set the bowl back on the mantle. She went into her kitchen and got a bowl from the open shelf and walked down the path with Flora. They picked and ate a few berries as they talked. Flora stopped and pointed in the direction of the rattlers, gave her friend a hug, and turned toward home. Emmy began picking berries and called to her friend, "Cobbler sounds good. I'll pick this bowl full for supper."

Isolated

Allen hadn't met anyone except the McCords when he started to work for Mr. McCord. He did not venture off the family property. He'd seen the bootleggers who lived in the woods. He felt isolated. He had his parents and work, work, work.

Jeb and Ted McCord were very quiet and seemed to resent this newcomer who knew nothing about lumberjacking. Allen had to be told how to do everything.

His clothes, yes, he wore blue jeans, but his jeans looked like they had just been purchased. Their jeans were worn with patches at the knees. His t-shirts had no stains, tears, or frayed edges. Their hands were calloused. Allen's were soft like a woman's hands. He stopped wearing gloves when he worked, in hopes of toughening up the skin on his hands. He began wadding up his t-shirts and jeans before putting them on. He took his jeans outside and rubbed them against the rough logs of the cabin to make them look worn.

At lunchtime on the job, Allen tried sharing his life in West Virginia. He told them of riding his bike, fishing, and just hanging out with his friends. These mountain brothers worked or hunted game. They had never owned

119

or ridden a bike or had leisure time to be with friends. They resented Allen. He quickly learned not to share his life in West Virginia. He ate his lunch in silence and listened to what those around him said instead.

The mountain people had a twang in their speech and left off the endings of words. When Allen spoke, he pronounced the whole word. Yet another reason he said little.

Allen worried about starting school where everyone spoke with the mountain twang. *Would the teachers also speak like that?* he wondered. So far, at work and at church, the youth his age kept their distance. None were willing to include him. He thought to himself, *If they are so different in character and interest, what will school be like? Will there be advanced math and science classes? I've always made good grades and taken the hardest classes. Will these classmates resent me? I know I have to ride the school bus to school. I've felt the teens' animosity at church and work. Will I be bullied on the bus or in class?*

His father drove him to the school. While his dad filled out the paper to enroll him, Allen spoke up and asked, "Does this school have sports, advanced placement classes, foreign language, and a school counselor?"

The secretary handed Allen a packet and said, "This will tell you the classes offered and the bus schedule. The school does have a football team. One of our seniors drives the school bus to and from school and for the few events at other schools. One of our teachers has the dual job of teaching English and serving as school counselor half day."

Allen asked, "Do Jeb and Ted McCord ride the school bus?"

She replied, "Jeb has finished school and Ted quit school last year."

Allen had hoped he'd have someone he knew on the school bus. Life was different from his past home. He felt uncomfortable in Appalachia. He became more observant of the places and the people. He'd even noticed his parents were changing.

His dad and Mr. McCord were friends, not just boss and worker. He'd noticed his mother went to see Mrs. McCord often. They had developed a true friendship. He saw their worry lines disappearing. They were laughing every day about something. They had to work harder, yet seemed content. His mind was racing. *When I start school will I have friends? Will I be happy at this school?*

Josephine (Jo) La Russa Graven

An Unexpected Visit

Mr. McCord let Tom and Allen off by the hardware/post office on his way home. Tom checked the mail, read the note from Peter, and put it in his shirt pocket. He'd share it with Flora and Allen after supper.

Allen went into the general merchandise store and bought three sticks of butterscotch candy. Mr. McCord had paid them when he let them off. Allen realized it was his last day as a lumberjack. It meant the end of his earning his own money. He met his dad as he came out of the hardware store and they walked the mile up the mountain to the cabin. They commented about the changing color of the leaves and the cooler weather. Fall had arrived.

On their walk home and halfway up the mountain, they stopped to listen to the sounds and sight of birds migrating south. His dad looked from the sky to his youngest son and asked, "Allen, I know you took in the school facility, and asked questions about the classes, but I could also sense some hesitation about going to this high school. How do you really feel?"

Allen replied, "I am concerned about being accepted. The kids my age I've met at work and at church won't include me there. What will it be like when there is a whole school of them and only me that talks different, dresses different, has never had to work until this summer? Will I fit in? As for the classes offered, they are almost the same as they would have been this year in West Virginia."

His dad nodded. He knew it would take time for Allen to adjust to the change. As they turned into the moss-covered planks of their home, they got a whiff of the rabbit stew and berry cobbler and quickened their pace to the cabin.

Flora could smell the stench of sweat and tree resin as they came in the door. Tom came over with the fork he'd picked up by his plate and reached in the skillet for a piece of rabbit. Flora slapped his hand, curled up her nose and said, "You need a bath before you eat my cooking."

"Just one piece for your hungry, hardworking husband."

Flora took the fork from his hand and pointed toward the bathroom door as they both broke into smiles. Tom met Allen as he came in the kitchen rubbing his wet hair with a towel. He helped his momma put the food on the table and grabbed a piece of rabbit while she went to see what was taking her husband so long.

Tom was spooning the peas when he told Flora the news. "I've been offered a fulltime job with McCord. Most of the trees from the tornado have been sent to the lumber yard or sawmill."

With a puzzled look on her face and her fork in mid-air, Flora asked, "If the trees from that bad storm are cleared, why is he hiring you full time?"

Tom answered his wife, "His son, Jeb, joined the Marines last Saturday. He leaves for boot camp in South Carolina on the eighteenth. McCord is worried with war talk in Korea that he may be shipped there, if there is another war."

Flora said, "Emmy didn't mention anything about her son joining the Marines when I was over there the other day."

Tom replied, "He intends to tell his mother tonight at supper. As for McCord hiring me full time, he got a government contract to clear the trees for a new mountain parkway from Lexington to the Kentucky-West Virginia state line. He has hired a team of men to clear the timber from Lexington to Mount Sterling and I will work on the work crew to clear the land from Mount Sterling to the state line. We will begin clearing in about a week.

"It will mean I will be away some when the weather is good, and not working for a few months if it is an unusually hard winter. It will take at least a year to remove all the trees and another two years to prepare the land for paving."

Allen beamed and spoke up. "He offered me a job this fall, too. When the tobacco he has growing on his property is ready, it will be cut, bundled, and hung in the tobacco barns to dry completely. With Jeb gone, he will need an extra hand for a few weeks. Mr. McCord said school is closed during the two weeks of tobacco harvesting."

After supper, Flora took her shawl off the hook by the door and wrapped it around her as she joined her husband and son on the porch. She sat in her rocker and used her foot to push it back and forth as the crickets serenaded them. Flora had her eyes closed when Tom took the postcard from Peter out of his pocket and said, "We got a postcard from Peter today."

Flora stopped rocking and opened her eyes as her husband handed her the postcard.

> "Dear Momma, Dad and little brother, College is harder than I expected. Working with the horses is also more intense than I expected, but I am enjoying both school and my job. On Sunday, the college cafeteria serves only breakfast and lunch. I have supper and fellowship at the Methodist church. Miss all of you.
> Love,
> Peter"

Flora sat there with the postcard in her hand then pulled it to her chest.

Tom watched his wife then asked, "Would you like to go there on Sunday after church? You could fix his favorite foods and we could have a picnic under that big tree he has written about to us."

Flora looked at her husband with tears in her eyes and nodded her head up and down for yes.

*****

Sunday morning, Flora dressed in a homemade dress and her everyday shoes. Tom and Allen were dressed in jeans and work boots. The congregation was still skeptical of the "Newcomers". They didn't share a pew, but left one empty.

After the service, Tom spoke with several men before he climbed in the truck and started the engine. Allen waited for his mother and helped her climb in the truck, then he got in the truck and stuck his head out the window to catch the breeze as his dad started down the mountain for the two-hour ride to Blyne.

Peter saw his father's battered truck parked in front of Yocum House when he returned from the library around one o'clock. He ran to greet them as they climbed out of the truck. His momma was crying and laughing at the same time as she hugged her son. He took them into the living room of Yocum House as he and his brother ran upstairs to put down his notebook and stack of books.

His parents looked around at the furniture and lamps in the parlor. There were several red-leather overstuffed sofas and a few end tables with grungy lamps in the bare wood room. Flora walked across the hall and peeked into the dining room. It was modestly furnished with a wide black table and eight chairs on each side of the table. There weren't shades on the two single windows. She was returning to the living room as her two sons bounded down the stairs.

The family walked across the street to the park as Peter grabbed the basket of food from the truck bed. They sat under the huge Osage orange tree with its long thick branches reaching the ground. Even though Peter had already eaten, he devoured his mother's cooking. He saw the tin of sugar cookies and grabbed a few.

After they had eaten, Peter showed his family the shops around the town square and the side streets. All the shops were closed on Sunday, but Flora wanted to go back and take a closer look at what they had for sale in the windows. Tom took his wife's hand and they walked back uptown, while Peter took Allen to see where he worked.

*****

Peter and Allen walked to the farm and Peter pointed out the deep blue-green grass and the horses grazing in the fields by the white stables. He told his younger brother about them. He said, "Those are racehorses. They live in those stables. They have an overseer to maintain all of their care. He and his family live in that little white house near the stables. There is a trainer who lives upstairs in one of the stables. He does the day-to-day care of the stables and exercises the horses daily."

Peter motioned for his brother to look at the fields of crops as they climbed further up the farm road. Peter said, "This is the part of the farm where I work. That big red barn is where the workhorses are housed and I care for them. "

Peter opened the door to the barn and Allen jolted back at the change in the fresh smells outside to the strong odors inside. There was the sweet smell of the fresh hay in the stalls. The pine bark under the bed of hay had a winter-green smell. Both absorbed the strong odor of horse urine and horse droppings. Peter opened a wooden box that held cloths, soap, ammonia and liniment to rub on them. Long leather gloves hung on a rack nearby. Bits and harnesses hung on the wall near the doors.

Peter told his brother, "I sing to them and they like it."

Peter reached into a huge barrel and took a handful of oats, handed them to Allen, and took another handful for himself. As they walked past the stalls to leave, the horses moved to the rail, tails switching, and put their heads out to get a few oats and be patted by Peter and Allen. Allen filled his lungs with the outdoor air.

Peter laughed at his brother's reaction and then said, "I had to get used to the smell of pine shavings, sweaty leather, hay, and especially the smell of horse urine. After a few days working, I got used to the smells when I raked out the stalls and laid fresh pine bark, shavings, and hay in each. When the horses are brought in from the fields, I wash them down, rub liniment on them, and give them their oats and water."

Peter and Allen walked back to the park, got a sugar cookie, and stretched out on Momma's patchwork quilt. They looked through the branches at the bright sun overhead.

Allen said, "I start school on Monday and I am not sure what to expect. The teenagers I've met at church seem to resent me and don't include me at the church socials. The two McCord brothers are so quiet and I found out neither of them attend school. I will have to walk a half mile down the mountain to catch the school bus."

They had only been back at the park a short while when they saw their parents walking hand in hand down the grassy knoll. Allen and Peter stood and folded the quilt. Allen started to put the tin of cookies back in the basket when Flora said, "Those are for Peter to keep."

Peter walked his family back to the truck and reached up to ruffle his brother's hair as they both laughed. He shook hands with his dad and gave his mother a long hug. He watched as they drove away. He had an empty feeling inside him as he saw his dad's truck disappear at the bend in the road.

Appalachian High School

Allen was apprehensive about starting school. He'd rubbed his blue jeans against the rough wall of the cabin. He'd even soaked them in lye water to make them look worn. His momma suggested he wear one of his shirts with a collar and an icon on the pocket. He rebelled and wore a gray t-shirt instead.

He debated putting his binder with the pocket for pencils inside his book bag or just carrying it in his hand. He reasoned with himself that probably the other students wouldn't have book bags, and decided to rough the binder on the bark of the oak tree beyond the moss-covered planks before walking down to the bus stop. He put on his work boots.

Allen took his lunch out of the lunch box he'd used in West Virginia and put the two sandwiches in a paper bag that nails came in from the local hardware store. He left the slice of pound cake in the lunch box. He didn't think anyone attending this school would have cake at lunchtime. He did everything he could to be like the boys on the mountain.

He picked up his lunch sack, waved to his momma, and walked toward the road. He went to the big oak tree and scraped the binder against it until it had scratches all over it. He was determined to add more scratches, then walked the half mile to the bus stop. He could hear the grinding of brakes as the bus came to a stop.

He said good morning to the bus driver, who did not acknowledge his greeting. He started to walk down the aisle in search of a seat. He was halfway down the aisle when a burly fellow stuck his foot out in the aisle, tripping Allen. He picked up his binder and lunch sack and went to the last seat on the bus. When the bus got to the school, he waited until everyone else was off before he got off.

The only seat in his first class was at the back of the room. No one acknowledged his presence. Just as it had been at church and on the bus, the students spread out and left no room for him. He sat alone for weeks. Few spoke to him during his first week. They just stared at him or tried to trip him. Over time, he sat with others, but they didn't include him in the conversations.

It took weeks before he felt comfortable enough to answer questions in class even though he knew most answers. It was not until he helped a few classmates with difficult math problems that they became his friends.

When his parents asked about school, he replied that he was getting used to it.

Allen had been assigned a study hall that he felt was a waste of his time, so he asked the counselor if he could add another class. Adding an academic class like chemistry would require him to do extra reading and class assignments to catch up. The counselor recommended the art class. Allen had never had an art class but thought it would be better than sitting in a study hall.

Allen used some of his money he'd saved in the coffee can to buy two sketch pads and artist pencils. The class was doing still life drawings at the time he entered the class. At first, his sketches were crude. Mr. Willard, the teacher, explained the techniques of form and shading.

At home he sketched a drawing of the lamp in the living room with its different shadows against the shade when it was on.   He sketched the kitchen table with wildflowers in a jar that his mother had picked.   Every night he spent an hour or two drawing.

The first two weeks of October, the school was closed for tobacco harvesting. Allen worked every day of the harvest. He worked alongside his dad, Mr. McCord and his son, and several others. They hung the cut tobacco from the rafters of the tobacco barn and opened the shutters for ventilation. The other students working for Mr. McCord noticed Allen worked as hard as they did and understood the job. They began to include him at lunch break and in the conversation.

Every night he sketched the men cutting tobacco, binding it, bending over with arms full, and others hanging it on the rafters. He applied all the techniques Mr. Willard had demonstrated in class. He added shading and facial features to make the drawings realistic.

When school was back in session, he brought his sketch pad of drawings and showed Mr. Willard.   He was impressed with Allen's drawings and gave him advice on techniques to enhance them.

Art—the Medium to Acceptance

The art class began drawing people. Allen was intrigued by the possibility of drawing people, adding details and shading to bring the art to life. He listened to Mr. Willard's comments and observed as he demonstrated the different facial shapes: oval, round, pear, and square.

The teacher selected three students to sit on stools at the front of the classroom and told the rest of the class to select one of the models to sketch. Mr. Willard talked about the shape of the face, high cheekbones, length of the face, shape of the eyes and color of the eyes.

Allen selected the girl with long black hair named Alecia. She caught his attention because of her quiet demeanor and her black hair that framed her oval face. Her almond-shaped eyes were green. He couldn't take his eyes off her. He noticed the cute curled nose she had and her pretty milk-white complexion.

Mr. Willard said, "Class, look at your subject. What do you see? Pale and lifeless first, then add depth, add shading, and make the face come alive with details."

Allen sketched Alecia's oval face and almond-shaped eyes. He studied her nose and lightly drew it in pencil, erased it, then drew it again, and again. He lost sight of her nose and just stared at her.

She was aware of his stares and darted from the stool when the bell rang, grabbed her books, and disappeared up the stairs to her next class.

Art was the only class Allen had with Alecia. He wanted to know more about her, but felt his staring scared her off. He took his sketch pad home that afternoon. He wanted to work on his drawing. He was intrigued by her.

After supper he excused himself and said he had to work on his assignment. His parents looked at each other, puzzled by his comment. He had never brought home homework.

His dad asked, "Are you having trouble with algebra or biology?"

Allen replied, "No, sir. I'm trying to express facial features in my drawing. Mr. Willard went over facial features today in class. I tried in class, but the face is flat. I want to read over my notes again."

"You take notes in art class?" his father asked.

"Yes, sir. My teacher explained we need to take one facial feature and make it stand out. I don't have the focus yet."

"Well, go draw, son, but don't stay up too late."

He completed his sketch the next day. Mr. Willard did not ask the models to sit again and that pleased Alecia. She moved two rows behind Allen, so he couldn't stare at her. He didn't need to stare at her. Her face was imprinted in his mind. She avoided him and darted off each time he approached her.

Every night he refined the sketch. He filled his pad with different degrees of perfection. He had finally captured her oval face as white as flour. Her almond-shaped eyes had specks of gold like the rays of the sun. The nose still puzzled him. If she would only smile, his sketch would be realistic and refined.

Every day for a week the class worked on perfecting their drawing. Mr. Willard walked from student to student, making suggestions on improving their sketch. When he looked at Allen's sketch, he made no suggestion. He smiled and patted Allen on the back.

On Thursday, Mr. Willard gave the class a homework assignment. He said, "Class, by Monday I want a basic sketch of your mother. Then you will have a week to create a detailed sketch. Apply the techniques we've discussed in your drawings. Observe your mother as you did with the class models. Take your sketch pad home every night and refine your drawing."

Josephine (Jo) La Russa Graven

How About Tomorrow Night?

At supper that night, Allen told his momma about his assignment to sketch her, then go back and add details. His comment surprised and delighted her. She had a big smile on her face when she answered him. She said, "How about tomorrow night? I'll wash and roll my hair and put on that new dress I made for church."

"Momma, it should be a natural sketch, the way you look every day," Allen said.

Flora washed and pinned her hair the next morning. She kept looking at herself in the mirror. "I've got bags under my eyes and my face is too thin. I need some color in my face. Maybe Emmy can help."

She walked over to her friend's house with a scarf tied around her pin-curled hair. Emmy was working on her clay bowl when Flora called to her, "What are you making now?"

Emmy set the clay bowl down and replied, "I'm still making clay bowls."

Flora asked, "Don't you have enough bowls?"

"These are for the big weekend festival in Blyne," Emmy said, as she looked up and saw Flora with a scarf tied around her head. She asked, "Is Tom taking you to a dance tonight? Why do you have your hair in bobby pins?"

Flora chuckled and said, "No, it is nothing like that. It is an art assignment for Allen. He has to make a detailed drawing of me tonight."

Emmy asked, "How can I help?"

"Be honest, Emmy. How does my face look? There are crow's feet around my eyes and creases around my lips. Do you have any face powder, rouge and lipstick that I could borrow?"

Emmy shook her head and commented, "He isn't going to notice that. What he will see is the sparkle in your eyes and your love for him. Take your hair down. Be yourself."

Allen came straight home from school and had his sketch pad swinging in his hand and a big smile on his face. He ran up the porch steps and burst into the kitchen where his mother was cooking.

He gave his momma a big hug and asked her, "Are you ready for me to draw you?" Flora put down the spoon she had in her hand, turned around to face her son and said, "I told you tonight, and it isn't night yet. You can draw me by the fireplace."

He helped his mother set the table and watched her as she busied herself at the stove. He noticed her skin had a warm glow, a soft peach color. Her big brown eyes were the feature he'd use as his focal point. After supper, he cleared the table while his parents sat by the fire and spoke in soft voices. He got his sketch pad and art pencils from his room. He moved a kitchen chair, so he had a clear view of his momma by the fireplace, then asked, "Are you ready, Momma?"

Flora patted her son's arm as he moved her closer to the fireplace. Allen sat at the kitchen table and drew a round face. His dad pulled up a chair behind him. Allen didn't say a word. His face was intense as his finger clutched the art pencil and began to fill in features. His dad was amazed. His son had artistic talent that had been hidden all these years. Flora wanted to see, but Allen kept saying, "I'm not finished yet."

Tom had been hovering over his son's shoulder and chimed in, "We'll have it finished tomorrow night."

Flora sat up straight, looked at her husband, and said, "Tom Cole, you aren't doing my picture."

Tom grinned, then burst out with laughter. Allen had the basic features drawn and closed his sketch pad and went to his room.

His mother went to change for bed. She whispered to her husband as she crawled into bed, "Have you noticed? He's changing. His voice is deeper, his shoulders are broader, and he has fuzz on his face."

"I've noticed. He is almost a man." Her husband turned off the lamp and kissed his wife good night.

Allen worked on the drawing all day Sunday and showed his mother and dad after supper. Tears filled

Josephine (Jo) La Russa Graven

Flora's eyes as she grasped her son's arm, then hugged him. Tom stood behind her and put his arms around her waist and she leaned into him.

Allen had captured the gentle creases by her eyes caused by her smile. Wisps of hair stuck out by her ears. Her smile was warm. Her eyes … her eyes seemed to draw a person into the picture. The eyes seemed to follow a person, no matter how the individual looked at it. Her eyes, big and brown, caught the flicker of the fire and seemed to cast shadows in them.

Flora held the picture and asked her son, "Will Mr. Willard give it back?"

"I'm sure he will," Allen replied.

Flora looked from her son to her husband and said, "I want to frame it and hang it over the fireplace."

Explanation, Romance and the Pest

Two weeks later, Mr. Willard had his students hang their two pictures side by side on the rope line with clothes pins, then explain what they had tried to capture. Mr. Willard called Allen last.

Allen placed his sketches of his momma first, then the drawing of Alecia. He explained, "In both subjects, I looked at their features. I looked at my momma's face as I always do, but then I noticed what big brown eyes she has. The flickering of the fire seemed to give movement to them. Unless I point it out, you might not notice the small creases at the corners of her eyes. They stand out more when she smiles, as she was in this sitting."

Mr. Willard kept nodding and smiling as Allen gave his presentation. He asked, "And what about your sketch of Alecia?"

Allen said, "I immediately saw the oval face and drew an oval. Her eyes are almond shaped which I noticed before, but I never really looked at the color. They are green with rays of gold like the sun."

The class and Mr. Willard turned to look at Alecia as she quickly pulled her head down. The teacher walked

143

over to her and, with his finger, he lifted her chin so he and the class could see her eyes.

He commented, "You're right, Allen. I hadn't noticed. Good observation and description."

Allen continued, "I originally planned to make her small nose the focal point. I sketched it and erased it many times. I kept looking at her nose, but couldn't get it right. I'm sorry, Alecia. I know you were uncomfortable with my staring."

"Good job," the instructor said, and gave Allen a pat on the back.

The class ended and Alecia waited at the door for Allen. "Thank you. May I have the sketch after Mr. Willard grades it?"

He looked at her, lost for words, then stammered, "Yes."

Allen was the shy one now. It took him a couple of minutes before he could look at her and asked, "Will you go to the school's fall dance with me Saturday night?"

She hesitated, then replied, "I'll let you know tomorrow. I have to ask my parents."

He walked her to her next class. They paused at the door and they both smiled. The bell began to ring, so he dashed to his next class and in through its door as the bell stopped ringing. His heart was singing. Alecia might go to the fall dance with him. He sat through the rest of his classes, but his mind was on her.

The next morning, she told him her father said no. That answer deflated him, but he understood. He was new and her parents knew very little about him or his family.

Allen began walking Alecia to class after he shared his drawing of her, and they began eating lunch together. A guy from another class always sat at their table and constantly interrupted their conversation. They moved to another table, but he moved, too. Every time he saw Allen walking with Alecia, he'd push them apart and start talking to Alecia. This went on for several weeks.

Allen had enough. Tempers flared and words turned into blows. A crowd of students, mostly guys, circled the fighters. Punches were thrown until the principal and a male teacher broke up the fight and the jeering students scattered. Both were suspended for three days. Allen had a black eye, bloody nose and split lip. He'd gotten his licks in, too, though the other fellow didn't look as bad as he.

His mother was horrified when she saw Allen's face that afternoon. He reassured his mother he was all right. His anger with the pesky guy had resolved the annoyance with the fight over his attention for Alecia. His dad said he didn't approve of fighting to resolve a problem, but he understood. It might help other students respect him and felt Allen's suspension was punishment enough.

When Allen returned to school, the students became friendly and included him. He'd shown he was tough enough to be a mountain boy. No one questioned his attention to Alecia after the fight.

In art class, Mr. Willard told Allen he wanted to submit his drawings of his momma and Alecia at the county fair art exhibit in the spring.   Allen told his parents some of his art had been selected to compete in the high school art competition at the county fair in April, but Allen didn't tell them what art.

Peacefulness on the Mountain

The leaves spiraled down to the ground—yellow, red, orange, brown and green. Mother Nature began ushering in the colder weather and preparing nature for its winter sleep. The early morning frost disappeared and sunshine replaced it.

Flora finished cleaning the kitchen and went out on the porch with a leftover biscuit to feed the birds. She broke off pieces and threw them just below the steps and watched as the birds fluttered above the crumbs. They waited until the blue jay had eaten before other birds flew down. This had become a Saturday morning ritual of saving one biscuit to share with the chirping birds.

Her husband came out a few minutes later with their second cup of coffee and sat beside her on the porch swing. He smiled at her as he handed her the steaming coffee. Tom pushed the swing back and forth with his foot and said, "You seem at peace here now, not anxious as you were when we first moved here. Your childhood memories of living here had you so uptight."

She moved a little closer to her husband and replied, "I'm happy here. It is peaceful, not like the stresses of my childhood in this cabin or our life in the city, especially that last year." She shivered and pulled her sweater closed.

He could see the steam from her coffee and said, "You're chilly. I'll get the quilt off the sofa and I can snuggle with you under it."

He stood and Flora pulled him back down with a giggle. "I'm not cold. The shudder was thinking of all the uncertainty of losing your job, losing the house, having to move here, Allen starting school here and facing some of the same problems of acceptance I faced as a child. Allen has experienced some of the same anxieties I faced. He's been uprooted from the only place he'd ever lived, lost his friends, had to give up his bike, and had problems being accepted here. He has been in this high school two months and is starting to fit in.

"Tom, were we so focused on materialistic things that we lost sight of what should have been important—family and God? Maybe we needed to be humbled."

Tom realized the mistake of overspending had led to their present circumstances. They sat there in silence as he looked out at the dirt drive, the trees blocking the view of the road, and then he turned and looked at his wife. He said, "That's all behind us. As your granny used to say, 'When God takes something away, He always has something better in store for you.' I know those aren't her exact words, but close enough.

"I couldn't find work in Huntington, but here a tornado provided the means of steady employment as a lumberjack. The people at church are friendly now. Allen is making friends and seems happy with the new school. He has discovered art and is good at it. Mr. McCord hired him to clear the downed trees after the storm and to work during tobacco harvesting. He promised him work next summer. It has helped Allen mature.

"You have Emmy as a friend and I have Michael McCord as a friend and boss. McCord is a fair man. He and I work together. I now have a job for at least the next three years as we work to clear the land for that mountain parkway.

Sometimes I miss living in Huntington and enjoying our life there before the layoff, but I don't want to go back. I think I have told you before, my daddy used to say, 'Running water doesn't run backwards.' Today, I understand what he meant. You can't go back. It is never the same."

Tom took the cup from his wife and set it on the stump used as a table. He pulled her closer and gave her a kiss. He smiled at her and said, "When I compare our life in the city to our life here, I would rather be here in this peaceful setting with you at my side, watching the pecking order of the birds eating your leftover biscuit."

Blyne's Fall Festival

Flora had finished two small baskets by the last week of October. She put a cloth in one of the baskets and placed the pound cake she had baked in it. She had no intention of selling her baskets. She wanted to see how her weaving compared to the woven baskets in Blyne.

The town was full of people walking from one display to the next display, and buying leather goods, baskets, cloth weavings, walking sticks, and hand-carved instruments. She stopped at every booth to examine the handiwork of the many craftsmen. She watched as artists wove grass, vines and cloth into baskets. She was amazed at how fast they could work.

Flora saw a large assortment of baskets of different shapes, sizes and patterns on a grassy spot by the park. She wandered over and questioned the basket maker about the price of her wares. There was one huge basket made with a wooden frame and crocheted sides. The bottom had three pointed sticks. Flora asked how it could be used. The weaver explained the basket was called a three-goose basket. The three sticks underneath were used to prod the geese and keep them together. The smaller baskets Flora had seen were selling for $5 and $10.

She picked up the three-goose basket and studied how it was constructed. The vendor said the basket was for sale and was only $35. Flora gently set the basket on the grass and left. She thought, "Crochet and wood ... with practice I could make one like that."

Flora stopped by Emmy's open tent and looked at all the baskets, dishes, bowls and vases she had made. There were four other people in the open tent with objects for sale. Emmy motioned for Flora to come up to her and whispered, "Sales have been good and this is just the first day. Next year, you could have a booth full of baskets and wreaths to sell."

Flora watched a woman at a loom. Her fingers guided the paddle as she peddled the loom frame back and forth. Flora had never seen a person weaving thread into cloth. She moved to the next shop and saw a potter molding clay into a bowl. Flora was fascinated by all the items on display. She didn't buy anything. She just looked and got ideas.

*****

Tom wanted to see the wood carvings, furniture, musical instruments, and the walking sticks. He examined the carved birds and watched as the artist used fine metal tools to create the feathered wing. He shook his head in disbelief at how realistic this man's creations were. He looked at the furniture crafted by Quakers—simple, yet beautiful. It was the choice of wood and the grain that gave it beauty. Twisted pieces of wood were used to create other items. Tom thought about the downed trees, the twisted limbs left by the tornado. Could he make something out of the castaway remains of that storm?

He'd never seen anything like this in West Virginia. The lap harps he knew he could make. He'd just have to play with the metal strings to make the musical cords. His mind was a buzz of ideas. It was the walking sticks that fascinated him. Some were straight with a shiny finish and others were entwined with twisted vines. He had never thought about a hobby until today. He spoke to one of the old gentlemen slicing away the wood as the group talked about their farms, their children, and the price of tobacco.

They'd stop occasionally to spit out the tobacco juice from the wad in their mouths. One old man wearing bib overalls and a tattered ball cap was doing most of the talking.

Tom decided he was the one to ask about whittling. "Sir, may I ask a question?"

All the men looked up, but the fellow in bib overalls who sat in front responded. He looked up at Tom and said, "If you is a mind to."

All the whittlers stopped and waited for Tom's question.

Tom said, "I've never done whittling before. I've never had time. How do you know what piece of wood will be good to use to make a walking stick?"

The old man asked, "You're a city fellow, ain't you?"

Tom grinned, then said, "I guess I was until a year ago. Lost my job, lost my home, and had to move to my wife's grandparents' old log cabin above Buck's Hollow."

The bearded gray-haired man put down his knife, let the stick rest against his fat belly, and shook Tom's hand. He asked, "Where you from?" as he released Tom's hand.

Tom replied, "We live near Majestic, Kentucky. My wife, our youngest son, and I came to see the craft show and to visit our son, Peter, who goes to Blyne College. Now I work my land and do lumberjacking on that new highway being built between Lexington and the Kentucky-West Virginia state line."

The old man, a local farmer asked, "How big is your farm?"

Tom said, "Four acres."

The others sitting on the porch began to laugh. One old codger, still laughing and slapping his leg, said, "That ain't a farm. That's a home place."

The others poked at each other and laughed even harder. The old farmer with glasses on the edge of his nose glared at Tom and asked, "You got any other questions?"

Tom nodded and said, "Yes, I do. How do you start? How do you know what wood to use?"

Yet another fellow called out, "You use whatever you find. I prefer hickory, black walnut, oak or ash."

Tom wanted to know more. "Do you cut pieces of wood to make them?"

The fellow in bib overalls said, "Sometimes I trim off an end or smooth out knots. When I see a limb or fallen branch that looks useful, I throw it in the corner of my barn and when I can, I work on it."

Tom asked, "Is that a pocketknife you are using?"

"Yep," they said in unison. "You got one?"

Tom pulled his from his pocket and clicked it open. All the whittlers leaned forward to see.

The old farmer in bib overalls said, "Leroy, hand me one of those sticks behind you."

The old farmer took the stick from Leroy and sliced away wood from the stick, looked at Tom, and asked, "You come here often?"

Tom said, "No, we've been here only one other time to see our son. Our neighbor told us about the fall festival. My wife wanted to see all the crafts."

The farmer continued, "Your wife got a name?"

Tom chuckled. "Flora."

The stick was given to Tom, and the old man said, "Sounds like you folks are settling in these hills."

Tom took the stick and began to whittle.

The Grassy Knoll

Allen left his parents and met his brother, Peter, to explore the exhibits at the fall festival. He asked his brother about the farm where he worked. On the family's first trip, he saw the working farm. Now he was curious about the race horses housed in the white stables with green doors. He had seen them grazing in the pasture of blue-green grass and asked Peter if he could see those beautiful creatures and their stables.

As they walked down the path to the white stables, a girl waved and Peter waved back.

Allen asked, "Who's that?"

Peter replied, "That's Maria, a girl in some of my classes. Her dad oversees the care for the race horses. They live in that house over there."

Peter continued, "Maria told me that while her dad is in charge of all aspects of the race horses' care, he has a trainer named Jake who has been the trainer for twenty years. I met Jake once when he was exercising the gray mare. He stopped at the white fence where I was standing and introduced himself. He let me rub the mare's head and neck."

157

Peter explained, "The race horse is built differently from the work horse. Race horses have lean bodies and thin legs. They are sired by other race horses and cost a lot of money to buy, train, and race."

The brothers cut across the pasture of blue-green grass toward the stable. Peter opened the door to the first white stable. Jake was grooming the big gray mare. He looked up and smiled when he saw Peter. The stable was immaculately clean. The smell of fresh hay and the clean smell of pine bark filled Allen's nostrils. Leather bits, bridles, and narrow saddles hung on the wall. Blankets with the farm's name on them were neatly stacked on a shelf.

Jake pointed to the stairs above the tack room and said, "I live up there. I have a bedroom, shower, and kitchen/living room combination; I need to be close to my horses."

Jake handed Allen and Peter a handful of oats for them to feed the five horses. The horses, seeing the oats in their hands, put their heads over stall gates and switched their tails as they munched. Peter and Allen patted them. The two brothers said their goodbyes and walked to the grassy knoll a distance from the crowd.

Peter asked, "What's your school like?"

Allen shared, "Most of the courses are the same as the ones back home. It is a county high school, so I have to ride the school bus. The bus has to pick up students from a lot of different bus stops, so it takes nearly an hour from my stop to the school. I had a problem with bullying until

I got in a fight and was suspended for three days. Momma was upset when she saw my black eye and split lip. Dad said maybe it was a way to be accepted. He was right.

"I was assigned a study hall when I registered for classes. It was a waste of my time. I asked for a change to a subject and was assigned art. I wasn't too happy about the change, but I knew it had to be better than study hall.

"Mr. Willard made it sound so good. I listened and took notes as he taught, then gave us a chance to sketch. I took some of the money I earned this summer and bought art pads and art pencils. I began to apply the techniques he explained as I sketched everything in sight.

"One day he demonstrated facial features. He talked about a focal point of drawing. He spent a class showing us how to accentuate a dominant feature. The next day, he had three students sit on stools. The rest of the class selected one model and sketched that person. We selected a focal point of our subject and were told to make our sketch come alive through that feature with shading and shape.

"I embarrassed a girl named Alecia with my staring. She avoided me until I did my presentation and explained my reason for staring. Now we are good friends and eat lunch together every day. The fight I had was with a pesky guy who was jealous that my attention was, and still is, given to Alecia. I walk her to class every day.

"After the fight, other students became friendly, and there has been no bullying. I guess I proved I am tough enough to be a mountain boy now.

"For the next assignment, we had to sketch our momma. I wish you could have been there to see Momma's expression when I told her. She rolled her hair the next day, borrowed make-up from Mrs. McCord, and put on a new dress she had made."

Peter asked, "What was Dad's reaction when he saw Momma?"

Allen laughed. "His face was one big smile, and Momma blushed. Then he gave her a kiss, wiped off the red lipstick and kissed her again.

"Dad sat behind me and watched everything I did. When I showed the sketch to Momma after it was finished, she said she wanted it framed and put over the fireplace when I get it back. I won't get it back until next spring. Mr. Willard is keeping both my picture of Alecia and of Momma. They know Mr. Willard is sending some of my art to the fair, but they don't know one of those pieces is the sketch of Momma. I want it to be a surprise next spring when they see it on display."

They changed the subject as their parents approached. Their momma was chatting away. Their dad had a slightly crooked stick in one hand and their momma's hand in his other. They spread the quilt on the ground and ate the chicken their momma had fried that morning, and they ate the rolls and pound cake she had baked the day before. A soft breeze cooled them, and a few dead leaves swirled around them as they enjoyed the afternoon.

Blinding Snowstorm

It was spitting snow when Tom climbed in his truck and headed toward the logging site. If they were lucky, they would get in a day's work before the heavy snows arrived. The radio announcer said the roads were clean. The snow accumulation would be no more than two inches by nightfall. A slight accumulation on the hood told him the weatherman's predictions might not be accurate.

When Tom left home, Allen was listening to the radio to see if school would be cancelled. He'd promised his dad he would not try to drive to school, but teenage boys don't always keep their promises. He prayed this was not one of those days.

Allen, afraid the trees would ice and fall, moved his car to the side of the house. He collected the eggs and brought in an armload of firewood, then went back for more firewood and stacked it on the porch.

Brushing snow off his coat as he came into the cabin, he asked, "Momma, I think it is going to be a heavy snow. What will happen to the chickens?"

"It isn't the chickens I'm worried about. It's your dad," his mother replied. Flora went back and forth from her housework to the window. The snow was nearly blinding and no sign of Tom. She muttered, "Where is he? Can he get home?"

*****

Tom had left a couple of hours earlier with light snow, but the weather had changed dramatically in those two hours. He traveled down the mountain in light snow, but it got heavier and heavier as he got to the main road. He knew he had to turn around before it got too deep to make it back up the mountain and too deep to see the road.

At that moment, Tom hit an icy patch, then heard the crunch of tires on the snowbank and felt the grip of the tires on snow. He looked up to heaven and said, "Lord, just get me to a place that I can safely turn around. There won't be any cutting of trees or loading of logs today. I can hardly see the road through this snow cover. Please, Lord, be with me today."

His hands gripped the wheel. His body was stiff. His eyes were glued on the sheet of white fluff with rutted edges. "Mind work, remember the curves."

He shifted gears as he came to the rise, but providence was not with him. His front tire went into the rut. He slammed his hands against the steering wheel and put his head over the wheel. He couldn't stay in the truck. He'd freeze to death. He got out of the truck and began his trek home.

The road began to glaze with ice. He slipped several times as he tried to climb the zigzagged road toward home. He shivered as the snow got deeper and the wind whirled around him. Tom pulled a half-buried leafless branch from the snow to keep himself upright. He had to drag his foot he'd injured years before. Tom was in immense pain.

Cold, wet, snow coated his face. He pulled his head down to try to see through the driving snow that made it impossible. Clumps of snow fell from his coat as he walked. His feet sank deep into the snow and the sucking hold took all his strength to pull his legs free. The winds seem to suck out his breath.

The slippery mountain grade caused him to fall several times. Tom was worried. He could not gage how far he had traveled up the steep mountain road. He had been struggling to climb up the mountain for what seemed like hours. The snow had become a blizzard, almost blinding him. He felt a raised bank and realized he was just below his home. The sound of wood against wood told him he was on the wooden planks that led to the house.

*****

Flora had watched the snow come down. She sent Allen to the wood bin to stack more wood on the porch. She put the plastic sheeting around the upper half of the half-wood half-screened porch, then moved the chickens into it. Allen helped her tack plastic over the windows and stuffed towels at the base of the doors to keep out the draft. She put a kerosene lamp on the table in case the lights went out, which they frequently did.

Their eyes searched for movement in the sheets of

snow, but saw none. Neither spoke, but both had the same thoughts on their minds. *Tom is out there in this blizzard. Is he safe? Is he trying to get home? Has he stayed at someone's home?*

With each sound outside of limbs cracking and crashing to the ground, they both ran to the window. Flora put on her largest soup pot and filled it with vegetables from her summer canning. She covered the pot and began to measure out the flour and corn meal to make a skillet of cornbread. She poured the dried milk powder into the measuring cup and added water. The granules did not want to dissolve. She held the cup in her hand, stirring as she looked out the window and saw movement. Flora looked a second time, straining to see what she believed was movement. She called to Allen, "Get your coat! I think that is your dad!"

Allen raced into the room putting on his jacket, and stopped long enough to take off his shoes and pull on his boots. He had his hat in his hand as he charged out the door. Flora hastily put the milk on the table, spilling it over the sides. She grabbed her coat and wool scarf, pulled the towel further away from the door and stood on the porch calling, "Tom! Tom! Is that you?"

She could no longer see any movement. Allen leaped from the porch into the deep snow, now covering the first three steps leading to the porch, and fell face first into the snow. He struggled to get to his feet and began to call, "Dad! Dad! Call out so I can find you!"

Tom was not sure he was hearing a voice or if it was his

imagination. He waited and listened, again he heard a faint voice. With all his might he yelled, "I'm beyond the planks."

Allen groped through the snow with his arms outstretched. "Dad! Dad! Can you hear me? Call out again!"

"I'm here, son."

Alan felt his dad's stiff coat. He yelled back to his mother, "He is here, but nearly frozen!"

Flora held the porch railing and sank deep into the snow, now up to her calves. She shuffled her feet through the snow to create a path. She sank her foot into the snow just in front of her last step. Allen was half dragging his father, half carrying him, by the time she reached them.

Flora put Tom's arm over her shoulder and they retraced her steps back to the house. Tom could no longer move his stiff legs and let them drag him through the snow. His coat was frozen to his body. Snow on the steps and porch parted like a shovel scraping a path as he was dragged into the cabin.

Flora pushed his chair close to the fireplace, while Allen held his dad. Together, they were able to ease him into his chair. There was an urgency in Flora's voice as she told her son, "Allen, get the quilts off the bed. Lay two on the floor and help me get your dad undressed."

Tears spilled from Flora's eyes as she looked at her husband shivering and his teeth chattering. It took both of them to get him from the chair and onto the pallet of quilts. He moaned as Allen and Flora removed his boots. His wool socks were dry and they left them on as they peeled away the soaked shirt, pants and underwear. Flora dried him with the softest towel she had. Allen took off the socks to find toes a ghostly blue. Tom cried out with each movement.

Flora told Allen to lay beside his dad as she got a basin of warm water and the flannel sheeting from her quilting drawer. She bathed his windburned, frostbitten cheeks with first cool then warmer water. She patted his whole body with the warm water until the frozen limbs could move. She raised his hips to slip on his underwear. Allen helped his mother raise his father's legs to get his pajama pants on, then lifted his shoulders up, so his flannel top could cover his chest. She buttoned it as he mumbled, "I love you, Flora. I didn't think I'd ever see you again."

Tears streamed down her face as she laid over her husband and just held onto him. He didn't have the strength to put his arm around her. She sponged his cracked lips with warm water until he could open them for the warm soup. She spooned the soup into his mouth and waited for him to open for more. His color was returning. He ate just the broth and drank half a glass of water then motioned that he didn't want any more. He was still shivering when he laid down in their bed. Flora piled quilts on top of quilts and crawled in beside him.

Allen replaced the towel by the door and soaked up the puddles of melted snow in the kitchen, banked the fire, then went to bed too. He tossed and turned. He could not get the picture out of his mind of his dad lying on the floor shivering. He took his sketch pad and sat in his dad's chair by the fireplace.

As the embers died down, he sketched what his mind would not let him forget—the frozen bluish toes, stiff and painful, the blood-red cheeks, the cracked lips, the melting snow on his eyebrows, and the pain in his dad's eyes that haunted him. He flipped the page and drew his mother as she moved over him with streams of tears pouring from her eyes.

Sometime after he had finished these, he was able to fall asleep. He slept in his father's chair with a quilt wrapped around his legs and his arms tucked beneath the puzzle of color his mother had made.

The next morning, Flora opened her eyes and saw the wall of white against the window. Glimmers of light created patterns on the bedroom walls. She turned to her husband. He was in a deep sleep and snoring loudly, which he never did before. She slipped from the bed, put on her quilted robe and went into the kitchen. Allen was still asleep in his dad's chair. He too looked exhausted.

She noticed the open sketch pad by the side of his chair and the two drawings he'd done during the night. He had captured the intensity of emotion in their faces and the anxiety of their body language. She closed the pad and set it back by the chair. If he wanted to share it with them, he would.

She looked out the front window. Snow was up to the porch. She reckoned it was at least two feet deep. Flakes of snow dropped from the trees. She turned and started a pot of coffee and put on a pot of water to make oatmeal. It was too cold to go on the back porch to get eggs. Besides, she thought, if there were any eggs, they probably were frozen. She filled her bowl with the creamy oatmeal, sprinkled cinnamon over it and added a tablespoon of brown sugar. She poured a cup of coffee and sat down facing the window. The only sound she could hear was the crackle of the fire and an occasional snore from their bedroom.

She lifted the covers and curled up next to her husband. He felt hot and clammy. He was wet with perspiration. She lifted the covers off of him and shook him. He responded with a moan, but did not wake up. Flora threw back the quilts and left just the sheet over him. She filled the basin with cold water and went back to bathe his skin with the cool water to bring down the fever. Over and over, she changed the water. She made strong tea and added honey. Tea and honey will cure anything. She gave him two aspirins, gave him water every half hour.

Then she remembered her grandmother use to make a salve and rubbed it on their chest and covered them with a cloth. What else did Grandma do for a fever? Think, Flora, think. She looked through the cabinets to see if anything came to her. She saw the pint of whiskey on the top shelf. She stood on her tiptoes and stretched as far as she could to get her fingers around the bottle. She poured a little in a cup, added black coffee, said, "What the heck," and filled it to the brim with whiskey.

Tom was cooler than earlier and wasn't sweating anymore. She helped him sit up and held the cup to his lips. He took a swallow and gasped as the stinging liquor coated his throat. He sat up straighter, turned to his wife wide-eyed, and asked, "Woman, what is this?"

"It's a hot toddy, Tom. You have a fever. My grandmother made one for us whenever we got sick. It always worked."

He asked, "Did you put the whole bottle in one cup?"

"Tom, you must be getting better, you're complaining."

He finished the hot toddy and passed out. Flora wasn't sure if it was the fever or drunkenness that caused him to sleep the rest of the day.

Even though the snow had quit, the wind howled all day. Drifts of snow covered the windows. She made bread, and then straightened her kitchen and living room. Flora kept looking out the half-glass back door at the chickens on the porch. They were all hunched together and not moving. She said to herself, *Just for a day. It is too cold for them to lay eggs. Besides, if the chickens freeze, we won't have any eggs."*

Allen woke up to the smell of bread baking and vegetable soup warming. He was scratching his head as he came into the living room and saw the chickens climbing on the furniture. He snickered, shook his head, picked up his sketch pad, returned to his room and closed the door.

Flora shooed the chickens off her quilting frame and

stitched for a while, that is until she heard Tom scream, "Flora, what are the chickens doing in bed with me? What crazy remedy is this?"

Flora shooed the chickens off the bed and said, "Tom, it isn't a remedy. It is just too cold on the screened porch for the chickens, so I let them inside."

She knelt on the bed, felt his forehead, and asked, "Are you feeling better?"

"Yes, but another one of those hot toddies might make me well and make it just like the other one."

Flora chuckled as she reached over to her husband and gave him a kiss.

"I'll have another one of those, too, and keep those dang chickens out of our bed."

Cabin Fever

It took two weeks for the snow to clear and life to resume outside. Tom and Allen used the time to sketch a new chicken house that would be attached to the cabin by a dog run. It would have hinged windows with wire screens. The window covers could be opened during the day and closed at night and during storms. Tom wanted no more chickens in his bed. They planned to build it in the spring.

Flora added, "While you are at it, you can build me a craft room off the kitchen. I've been saving my quilting money and basket making money to buy me a potter's wheel and a kiln. I could put my quilting frame and my sewing machine in there."

Tom asked, "What sewing machine?"

His wife smiled that sweet smile that she knew would melt his heart and said, "The one you are going to buy me when you finish my craft room."

Tom chuckled and went back to his drawing.

After days of gray skies, howling wind and blowing snow, they woke to sunshine streaming in the windows. Tom rolled out of bed and threw back the curtains to see streams of colored light against the glistening snow. He grabbed Flora by the waist and pulled her from the bed to see. At first, her body was like a rag doll, limp in his arms; then, fully awake, they were dancing around the bedroom in their nightclothes.

Tom said, "The sun is finally out! I can get outside again."

Flora remarked, "I thought you liked being cooped up with me."

"I do, baby, but you're wearing me out with this loving—day, night, as well as in between," he said, while laughing. "What's our son to think? He's got a pair of lovesick parents."

Flora pushed him away laughing and reached for her clothes. Tom snatched them away and pulled her back into bed.

Allen heard the squeak of the bed springs from his parents' bedroom as he headed to the bathroom. A smile danced across his face as he shook his head and mumbled, "They are at it again."

He went into the kitchen, stoked the fire in the wood-burning stove, then started the coffee. He had the bread buttered and was cracking the eggs when his parents appeared.

"You see the sunshine, son?" his dad asked.

"Yes, sir. I did. I wasn't sure you and Momma had, so I started my own breakfast. Coffee is ready. You want sunny-side-up eggs or scrambled eggs?"

Tom winked at Flora and said, "It's a sunny-side-up day."

She turned so her son couldn't see her blush.

The snow melted all that day, leaving long icicles hanging from the roof the next morning. They needed to clean off the melting ice and snow before Flora could throw out pinecones stuffed with bird seeds and coated with suet. By afternoon, animal footprints decorated the snow, the chatter of birds filled the air, large chunks of snow crashed to the ground, and melting snow dripped down the windowpane.

They moved the chickens to the plastic-enclosed back porch. Flora cleaned inside as Tom and Allen swept off the porch and used a snow shovel to clear a path from the porch and the wood pile. They worked outside most of the day. Or rather, they worked in between snowball fights. Flora smiled as she watched her men, and enjoyed their laughter.

Late in the afternoon, she went outside with a soup pot and a long-handled spoon to get fresh snow buried below the surface to make snow ice cream, as they bombarded her with snowballs.

As they peeled off their layers of clothes, Flora made the snow ice cream. Her son and husband sat at the table in anticipation of eating snow ice cream for their supper.

Christmas

Christmas had always been a special time in the Cole family in the past. Flora baked cookies and cakes to share with their friends. The little white church they used to attend had an indoor dinner on the last Sunday in winter, but at Christmas time they celebrated the Sunday before Christmas.

Several men from the church would go into the woods and cut down a fir tree and drag it to the room behind the sanctuary. The children threaded popcorn and red berries to hang on the tree. Mothers made circle ornaments to hang on the tree out of scraps of material left over from making clothes for their children. Families brought roasted meat, vegetables, bread and baked goods to share. They set the table as the older children hung the circles of color on the tree and the younger children danced around the tree with strings of popcorn, singing Christmas carols.

Mountain life was different. They hadn't lived there long enough to have a wide circle of friends. The Cole family were now accepted members of the church community. This church celebration was very different from what they had in West Virginia. It seemed more meaningful. The members came in their worn jeans, scuffed boots and homemade dresses. The only church decoration was a few leaves with big pine cones stuffed with red berries on all the window sills. After the service, everyone worked together. Everything on the tree was homemade. The food was simple and, other than a wild turkey, it was the same food they ate every day at home.

In Huntington, the Cole family would attend church service and then go home to celebrate with family. Dinner included many vegetables, a turkey with stuffing, canned fruit, homemade rolls, cookies, pies and cakes. Flora used her best tablecloth and fine china.

Flora wanted to share in Appalachia as she had for Christmas in Huntington, West Virginia. She baked for a week. She made gingerbread men for the twenty-four young children at church and a jam cake for the church dinner. Tom killed several rabbits and cleaned them. Flora made her large soup pot of rabbit stew and lots of mashed potatoes to share at the church lunch.

For the cabin, Allen and Tom cut down a small fir tree. Flora popped the popcorn in the wire basket with the wooden handle over the open fire in the fireplace. They sang along with the singer on the radio as they made popcorn chains and drank hot chocolate. Peter was coming home on the Trailway bus the next day, and Flora wanted everything ready for his arrival.

Allen drove down the mountain to pick up his brother. He wanted to show Peter his car. His brother asked him how he could afford a car.

Allen said, "You know the six weeks before school started, Mr. McCord let me work clearing the downed trees. I saved almost all of it, then he let me work the two weeks of tobacco harvest. It is an old car, a 1934 coupe, that a widow did not drive any more. It was just sitting in her barn. Dad checked it out and said it would be a good buy. It's smooth running, and I paid what the owner wanted.

"I didn't like riding that school bus to school. I didn't care for the bullies either. I was concerned about driving the car to school. I thought those bullies might do something to it or to me. Somebody put some scratches on the hood and let the air out of the tires once, but no one has bothered it since then."

Tom stayed home and helped Flora unpack the ornaments she'd collected through the years. They would decorate the tree after supper. She saved some of the ginger cookies she'd made for church for her family. Flora placed rolls and a pound cake on the china cabinet. She'd cut a paper bag into a string of bears and hung it on the china cabinet. Flora had Tom hang over the fireplace a wreath that she had made, just as Allen pulled into the yard. She ran to the door with open arms and a smile to greet her older son.

While they ate supper, Peter told his family about his classes and his final exams he'd just finished the day before he came to the cabin for Christmas break. He wouldn't know his grades until January, when the next semester began. He mentioned a girl in some of his classes and said they studied together and were dating.

His dad asked, "Who cares for the work horses during the Christmas break?"

Peter said, "Other fulltime workers share the care of the horses when school isn't in session."

Allen asked, "Is this girl you mentioned the one who waved to us when we came up to Blyne in October? She's cute."

Peter nodded and said, "Yes. Her name is Maria. As I said, we have some of the same classes together. Her family lives on the farm where I work. Her dad is in charge of the race horse part of the farm."

His momma asked, "You aren't spending all your free time with this girl and neglecting your studies, are you?"

Peter laughed. "No, Momma, we spend most of our time studying our class material. I promised you before I left for college, I'd study the books, not the girls."

After the supper dishes were washed and put away, they hung the Christmas ornaments on the tree. They sat in front of the fireplace with a plate of cookies and hot chocolate as Tom read from the Bible of Christ's birth. As the fire flickered, they sang "Silent Night," "Come All Ye Faithful" and "O' Come, O 'Come Emmanuel."

The two brothers stayed up late every night and shared how life had changed for each since the past summer, with the family move and Peter off to college.

Peter shared, "I miss being with the family, teasing you and being spoiled by Momma's cooking, but being in college and working is a way I can someday have a good job and a family."

Allen shared his sketch pads of drawings of animals in the snow, the men working during tobacco harvest, and his sketch of his parents when his dad had been caught in that blizzard.

He said, "Dad was almost frozen when he reached home. I wasn't sure he was going to live. He ran a high fever and Momma gave him coffee with whiskey twice. It did the trick. After he slept it off, he got better."

Allen laughed as he continued, "Momma let the chickens in the house and one climbed in the bed with Dad. He woke up and yelled at her 'What crazy remedy is this?' Momma shooed it out of the room and kept chasing the chickens off the table, the sofa and out of Dad's chair the rest of the day."

He told his older brother about sketching Alecia and their mother. "I embarrassed Alecia by staring, as I told you, but now she is my girl. The picture I did of her and the one of Momma will be sent to the fair in April for high school art competition. Don't say anything to Momma and Dad. They know some of my art will be entered, but not what pieces. I want it to be a surprise when they see Momma's picture on display. Mr. Willard, my art teacher, has hinted that my art is good enough to send to several art schools. He thinks I might get a scholarship."

Christmas morning, Flora got up very early and made cinnamon rolls for breakfast, then took the wild turkey Tom had killed out of the refrigerator and put it in the oven. She put her gifts of new knitted socks and a sweater for each under the tree. A large tin of cookies also was placed under the tree for Peter to take back to school.

Allen had made a picture frame and put a picture of his mother throwing pieces of biscuits to the birds hovering nearby. Allen went through the family album and found the picture of Peter and him swinging in the tire swings with big smiles and their feet pushing them. His dad just held it for a moment, remembering. He passed it to Peter, who smiled and said, "I miss those days."

Allen gave his brother a rabbit skin hat with flaps. Peter put it on and continued with the gift exchange. He handed his momma a box wrapped in shiny red paper. Flora put her finger under the edge of the paper and slowly pulled the box out. She did not want to tear the shiny paper. She could use it again. She opened the box and pulled the pottery vase from it and pulled it to her chest then ran over to Peter and hugged him. He gave his dad a new pocketknife and brought a pack of art pencils for Allen.

Tom used his new whittling skills to carve a small bird for Flora. He cleaned and oiled a used rifle he'd bought and a box of bullets. He'd been teaching his son, Allen, how to hunt for game.

Peter didn't see a gift from his dad under the tree. He looked up when his dad called him, to see the keys to his dad's old truck and a five-dollar bill for gas.

His dad said, "Mr. McCord was selling his 1940 truck. I put $100 down and McCord will deduct $5 a week from my pay until it is paid. I thought you might want a set of wheels."

Peter just stood there with his mouth wide open in disbelief.

On New Year's Day, Peter drove back to college with two sandwiches his mother made, a thermos of hot coffee, a tin of sugar cookies, and another bag of stamps and writing paper. Allen ran along the side of the truck until it turned out of the yard and started down the mountain.

Josephine (Jo) La Russa Graven

A Scream in The Night

On a warm late-April morning in eastern Kentucky, when Mother Nature awoke and the rooster crowed, Flora climbed out of bed and started breakfast. She had the coffee made and was flipping the pancakes when Tom came up behind her, kissed the top of her head, and reached for a broken pancake. In between bites he said, "Smells good in here, almost as good as you," as he leaned down and kissed her neck.

After breakfast, Flora went out to the chicken coop, looked at her brood, and decided which would be Sunday dinner when they visited Peter. She chased after the red one, cornered it, grabbed it by its neck, and swung it around to break its neck.

She opened the kitchen window, filled the sink with hot water and put the chicken in it. Flora plucked the feathers and washed the chicken. She took her cleaver and chopped it into pieces, then put it in a bowl of buttermilk and put it in the refrigerator. She made rolls and a pound cake after Tom and Allen went hunting.

Allen was on spring break and Tom had asked for the day off. It had been four months since the family had seen

Peter. She knew he was a man now, but in her eyes, he was still her little boy.

Flora walked over to Emmy's house after she finished her baking and housework. The redbud trees were in full bloom and she pulled small branches of flowers to put in the vase Peter had given her. She wanted to finish an oblong all-wood basket she had made, but she needed help finishing the edge.

Peter had told her at Christmas time that the bigger baskets sold for $10 or more in the shops. She had seen the expensive baskets when they visited Peter last fall. She thought with practice and Emmy's guidance, she could make some just as nice. She didn't intend to sell the finished basket, but she wanted to compare her workmanship to the baskets in the shops.

Emmy was rolling something gray on a big slab of concrete. As Flora emerged from the tree-lined path, she saw Emmy with something in her hands.

Flora called out, "What are you making?"

Emmy looked up from her rolling of clay, smiled and called out, "I'm making a bowl out of rolls of clay. I get my clay from the hardware store. It comes in a big plastic bag to keep moist."

Emmy rolled the clay strips, then placed them one on top of the other. After each, she moistened her hand and smoothed the coils with her hands. Flora didn't understand the process and continued to ask question. She asked, "Why the long coils?"

Emmy replied, "When I have enough ropes of clay, it will be a bowl."

Still puzzled, Flora asked, "Where did you learn to be a potter?"

With clay-covered hands, Emmy replied, "I taught myself. I bought a pamphlet for a dime that shows how to make coiled bowls and vases. I made that one sitting in the sun and I made that crooked neck one, too. I get a little better with each piece I make."

Flora was fascinated and asked Emmy if she would teach her.

Emmy smiled at the thought of sharing another skill with her neighbor and said, "I will."

Flora had her basket in her hands and pulled her arm up so Emmy could see it, as she asked, "If you have time, I'd like you to show me how to finish this edge. We are going to Blyne tomorrow to see Peter and I want to take this basket with me. He said they sell wooden baskets for $10 or more, depending on size. I want to see how mine compare. I don't plan to sell it."

Emmy nodded and went back to rolling clay chains and said, "When I have eighteen coils stacked and smoothed, I have a bowl."

She set the completed bowl in the sun with the others, washed her hands, and removed the clay-spattered apron before reaching for Flora's basket. Her friend took a piece of the narrow, thin, soaked wood and began to weave sideways around the basket. When Flora understood how to finish the basket, she took it from Emmy and began to finish the edge.

She left her friend to finish her bowl making and Flora went home to finish her basket. It took her several hours of tedious effort to complete the edge. She placed it on the mantel and hoped Tom and Allen would notice it when they came home. Flora had supper almost cooked by the time her men got home.

Tom remarked, "Long day." He took off his baseball cap and put his head under the kitchen faucet. The water ran through his hair and down his face. Flora stood beside him and handed him a dry towel as he raised his head. Allen disappeared into the bathroom to clean up before supper.

Flora set the table and put the food on it. She kept looking at the basket, undecided as to where to set it so her husband and son would see it. Allen noticed it on the mantel as he sat down to supper and he got up to get it. He asked his momma, "Is this the basket you have been working on for weeks?"

Flora beamed. Tom took it from Allen and examined it. He remarked, "It's very nice. What are you going to do with it?"

Flora waited a minute to respond, "I think I am going to admire it for a while."

All three laughed. Tom set the basket back on the mantel, then sat down to eat. They helped Flora clear the table, then Tom and Allen sat on the sofa to listen to the baseball game on the radio. By the time she had finished the dishes, they were both asleep.

Before going to bed, Flora packed the picnic basket with the rolls and pound cake. She turned the chicken in the buttermilk and turned off the light. The only noise she could hear was the static on the radio. She turned it off, then rubbed her son's shoulder and softly said, "Allen, go on to bed."

Her son stirred, looked up at his mother, then stumbled toward his room. Tom groaned, started to stand and headed for bed. He changed for bed and was snoring before she crawled in beside him. She started her nightly prayers but fell asleep while saying them.

A scream! A piercing scream like a woman afraid had Tom out of bed and at the window before Flora could sit up.

Allen rushed into the room with fear in his voice and said, "Mom, Dad!"

Tom shushed him and continued to look out the window. He saw the yellow eyes of the big cat as it tried to pounce on the chicken that had gotten out of the chicken coop. Tom got his rifle, opened the window, put the barrel through the window, and fired.

Allen just stood there and asked, "Did you kill it?"

His dad said, "I think I missed. Be careful when you are outside."

They tried to sleep but tossed and turned, sat up and listened each time they heard a noise. They slept late the next morning and Flora had to hurry to get the chicken fried and breakfast on the table before they could leave for Blyne. Tom stood on the porch and looked around to see if he could spot the big cat.

Allen helped his momma bring out the basket of food. Flora carried the wooden basket she had made and kept it in her lap. Tom drove slowly out of the yard and down the mountain. All eyes were on the wooded area.

Tom remarked, "We need to be home before dark and be watchful of that mountain lion. Allen, we have got to build the chicken house and your mother's craft room. We need to remove the temptation of wildlife killing our chickens."

Flora's New Interest

As the family drove to Blyne, they noticed that the trees had filled out with green leaves, while redbud trees and dogwood trees colored the mountain with flowers.

The work on the parkway had begun. The men had to stay in tents when working away from home, but they didn't have to work on Saturday or Sunday. Tom told his family that all the men who worked on the parkway were guaranteed a job after this project was completed to the state line. McCord's company would blast through the mountain and create a tunnel into West Virginia.

Flora was anxious about the possibility of Tom working with explosives. She had lost her father and her brother in coal mine explosions. She didn't want Tom or any other man hurt or killed.

Tom sensed her anxiety and changed the subject to her looking at baskets and comparing her workmanship.to that of baskets in the shops. Flora said she wanted to see coiled pottery as well as pottery made on a potter's wheel. She hoped there was a pottery shop with a potter at work.

Since Tom had seen the old farmers whittling in Blyne, he had dabbled at making walking sticks. He brought one he'd made from an elm limb that he felt had potential. He had his new knife in his pocket and hoped he'd meet the farmers again.

Peter met his family in the park and they shared lunch before each went off on their own adventure.

Flora put her wooden basket on her arm and walked uptown to the shops. She looked in every window and compared her workmanship to those in the shops. Flora kept looking for pottery. She turned down a side street and looked in a candle shop, a cloth weaving shop, and a leather tooling shop before she saw the pottery shop.

Flora stood at the storefront window and watched as the potter slapped the wet clay on the wheel. Water began to splash as he pumped the wheel. First, it looked like a long cylinder then it widened and bowed out as he guided it with his hand as it spun. Her head was bobbing up and down as she watched. *Yes*, she thought, *I can do that. I'll find a potter's wheel and there will be no more crude coiled bowls and vases. Someday, I'm going to have a potter's wheel.*

Peter and Allen stayed under the gigantic Osage orange tree and just talked. Allen told Peter of the mountain lion that screamed like a woman and the chicken it killed. He said, "During that winter storm, when we were cooped up in the cabin, Dad and I designed a chicken house and a craft room for Momma to be attached to the cabin by a dog run, but his work schedule hasn't left time to build it. He said we will start on it next week. Sometimes he has to work away from home and he doesn't want Momma, me or the chickens attacked by a mountain lion or a bear."

190

Peter told his brother, "I'm taking sixteen hours next semester. I don't think it will be any harder than taking thirteen hours. I've learned to balance my class time and studies, my work time and fun time. I have a nine o'clock date every night with Maria. Sometimes we study for a test or do an assignment together, stroll the farm or we sit on the swing by her parents' house and watch the stars."

"I thought you said she was just a girl in some of your classes. You made no mention of her as your girlfriend," Allen said jokingly.

Peter came right back. "Are you still chummy with that girl in your art class? What's her name? Alice? Angie? Agnes?"

Allen spoke up, "Yes, and her name is Alecia. There aren't any movie theaters or restaurants nearby, so we picnic down by the creek near the church or we sit in my car and talk when I bring her home after school. She is as good or a better artist than I am, my art teacher said. We plan to take art again next year and maybe have the same scheduled classes."

Tom found the old farmers whittling on the same porch as they had been on his original visit. He sat down on the porch step in front of them, took his knife out of his pocket, and began slicing long thin strips of wood off the limb he brought with him. He felt at home with the old men on the porch.

When he had finished smoothing the stick, he checked the time on his watch. It was three o'clock. He needed to locate his family and drive home before dark.

Josephine (Jo) La Russa Graven

And the Potter's Wheel Turned

Flora worked in the cabbage patch all morning. She arched her back and wiped the sweat off her brow. She pondered how she would spend the rest of her day and decided to visit Emmy.

As she came into the clearing, she called, "Morning, Emmy. Can you stand a little company? It gets lonely with Tom gone all week."

Emmy came out the kitchen door and hollered, "Come in. I'd love a little company, too. I've got a chocolate pound cake I just took out of the oven. It should be cool enough to cut by the time I brew some tea."

Emmy shared a note from her Marine son. His unit had been shipped to California. She said it would be at least another year before he'd get home for a visit. Emmy poured the tea and added ice as Flora sliced the cake.

Flora told her about the potter's shop and how easy he made it look to take a slab of clay and make a bowl right before her eyes. Emmy said she'd seen the man in the potter's shop work, but she'd also seen potters make things by hand that looked just as pretty.

Emmy set her plate down and went into the house. She came back out with two pieces of coiled pottery she'd made. The big bowl had streaks of dark blue to streaks of almost white as it circled the bowl. "I made this, and used blueberry juice and a paint brush to get the swirl effect. The coils of clay on this vase give it character. I used blackberry juice to add color. I don't think they look crude. Do you?"

"No, they are beautiful," Flora replied.

Emmy had shown Flora how to coil clay and make a coil bowl and a vase. Flora felt she had imposed on her friend by using her clay and potter's tools. She needed her own.

Flora asked, "Where do you buy your clay and where did you find potter's tools? Did you order them from a catalogue?"

Emmy replied, "The hardware store has the clay. I buy big blocks sealed in plastic to keep it moist. Are you sure you want to make pottery?"

Flora nodded her head and said, "Yes, you make it look so easy. I'd like to make more and get as good as you. Someday, I am going to own a potter's wheel. I'll save my basket weaving money until I can buy one. When you go into town again, can I go with you? I'd like to get a bag of clay and one or two of the tools you have."

The next morning, Emmy drove to the Cole cabin and honked the horn. Flora hadn't mentioned to Tom that she might spend the money she'd earned from selling her baskets at the mercantile store. She had $23 tied inside a handkerchief. She put the money in her purse and raced down the steps and into Emmy's blue Ford car.

Emmy parked in front of the hardware store and walked in as the bell above the door chimed. The merchant was waiting on another customer, so they walked around the dimly lit store with objects leaning against cases and shelves cluttered with everything from hammers to coffee pots.

After the other customer left, the merchant walked over to them. Emmy asked him about his wife and sons before she introduced him to Flora.

Emmy said, "This is my neighbor and friend, Mrs. Cole. Her family lives in that old abandoned cabin of the Tully family. They were her grandparents. Of course, they have really fixed up that cabin. Her husband works for my husband, Michael. I've shown her how to make clay bowls. She wants supplies to make her own."

Flora shared, "We have a son at Blyne College. When we visited, I watched a potter on a potter's wheel create beautiful pieces. I'm going to make coiled objects right now, but someday I am going to own a potter's wheel."

The owner of the store grinned and said, "I've got one in my storeroom. It needs a little work. Would you like to see it?"

Flora and Emmy followed him into the storeroom. He pointed out a detached leather strap on it. Flora asked the price and could he repair the problem?

He said, "No, I'm not a handy man, but your husband could fix it in a jiffy. It is a bargain at only $25. A new one would cost you $50."

She knew she didn't have enough money for the potter's wheel, clay and tools. Flora didn't want him to sell it to someone else, but she knew she'd have to have the clay and tools if she was going to make any clay objects. She didn't say anything, turned and walked out of the storeroom.

Emmy showed her the tools she needed, while the merchant brought out the ten-pound block of clay. He rang up the supplies. It came to $20.43. Flora took the handkerchief of money out of her purse and began counting it out. She stopped and asked, "Would you accept four baskets I made and all the money I have here and let me have the potter's wheel, too?"

He thought a minute, looked at her determined face and said, "It will depend on the quality of your work. You know I have to make a profit, too. When can you bring them in?"

Flora said, "I've got two made now, and I am making a third one. I could have the third and fourth ones finished in a couple of weeks."

The owner of the store said, "I can't promise anything. Bring them in. Maybe we can work something out."

The following Monday morning, Emmy took Flora and her two baskets to the hardware store. The balding, potbellied owner examined each. He knew he could sell them for $10. He told Flora he'd give her $5 each for the two baskets and he'd let her open an account for the balance.

She didn't know when she'd have another $10. It would take her weeks to make two more baskets. She was torn as to what to do. She kept looking at the storeroom door and back at him. Her lips were pinched in, and her hands twisting. Finally, she said she'd charge the $10 and pay him as soon as she could.

The merchant got a wheelbarrow and loaded the potter's wheel. The heavy wheelbarrow wanted to swerve and hit shelves as he wheeled it out to Emmy's car.

When Emmy and Flora got to the Coles' cabin, they had to figure out how they would get it out of the trunk and into the house. They tried getting on each side and lifting it out, but that didn't work. Flora thought maybe they should wait until her son came home from school, but that would inconvenience Emmy to drive back over. And she wouldn't know when Allen was home.

The McCords had a telephone, but Flora and Tom didn't. Finally, they decided to pull the old rusty wagon to the lip of the open trunk. They inched the potter's wheel to the edge of the open trunk and tugged until it fell into the wagon with a loud clatter. Now the problem was how to get it into the craft room Tom had built.

The chicken house and the craft room were connected by a dog run. The chicken house had a ramp that led to the outside fenced chicken coop. The outside coop had a gate. Flora rubbed her forehead and just stood there for a minute. Then she told Emmy of the ramp.

Flora and Emmy both pushed the wagon to the back of the cabin expansion. Flora let the chickens out. She and Emmy got a running start and rolled the wagon to the level floor, out the dog run door and into the door to her craft room. They tilted the wagon next to a wall and let the potter's wheel fall to the floor. Working together, they were able to right it.

Flora shooed the chickens back into their chicken house, and she and Emmy put the wagon back outside. She washed her hands and put on a pot of coffee. They sat on the porch with the steaming coffee. Flora thanked Emmy for taking her and for helping her get the potter's wheel from the car to the craft room.

Emmy asked, "What will Tom say when you show him the wheel?"

Flora said, "I think I'll cover it with a sheet and wait a few weeks before I tell him. Maybe by then I will have another basket made and have paid down the debt."

Emmy shook her head as she got up to leave. "I wouldn't do that. I'd be honest with him. If he gets angry, it would be better now than for him to find you have kept this a secret. But it's your life. Do as you want to do." She waved as she got in her car and pulled away.

*****

It rained that afternoon, so the men on the parkway project went home. The weatherman predicted heavy rain for the rest of the week. Tom was drenched when he came home and not in a good mood. Allen helped his mother clean the kitchen after supper, then went to his room. His mother had shown him the potter's wheel and he didn't want to be around when she told his dad.

After she had finished in the kitchen, she sat on the sofa with Tom and they listened to "Only the Shadow Knows" show. When the program ended, Flora got up, patted Tom's leg, winked at him and went into the kitchen. She fixed a pot of coffee and brought it to the living room. They listened to Bing Crosby and Tom sang along and Flora hummed. Her mind was racing. *How am I going to bring up the purchase of the pottery supplies and mention the potter's wheel?*

When she drained her cup of coffee and took both their cups to the sink, she whispered to herself, *It's now or never. You must tell him.*

Flora walked back in the living room and her husband patted the seat beside him as he continued to sing along with the radio.

She didn't sit down; instead, she stood in front of him and said, "I bought supplies to make pottery pieces like Emmy. I used the money I've earned from the baskets I've sold and that bunch of dried flowers I sold to that florist over in Weeksville.

"Tom, I also bought a potter's wheel from the man at the hardware store. It needs a little repairing, but I know you can fix it."

Her husband seemed extremely annoyed when he yelled, "Where did you say you bought it? And if you bought all these supplies," as he threw his arm out in the direction of the supplies on that makeshift table, "how did you pay for all of this? I know your basket sales wouldn't cover supplies and that … that broken contraption."

Flora said, "I bargained with the owner of the hardware store in exchange for the two baskets I had made and the promise to make two more to pay off my account. As I said, the potter's wheel needs a little work, but I know you could fix it. I used the money I had from other basket sales, and the dried flowers I'd sold to the flower shop, to buy the clay and tools I need."

In a loud voice he asked, "How much did all this cost?"

He paced the room. He picked up the tools and put them back down. He ran his hand across the bag of clay and the roll of cheesecloth. Flora didn't answer. She held her hands and her muscles in her arms tightened. She didn't want to tell him. She knew he'd be angrier. She said nothing.

He asked again, "How much did all this cost?" as he again waved his hand over the assortment of supplies.

Flora said in a very meek voice, "It is money I earned. I should have a right to spend it as I please."

"How much do you still owe him?" Tom snarled.

"I owe him $21.85 and I can pay him whenever I have the money. I'm not asking you to pay my debt. I'm asking you to look at the wheel and repair it. Is that too much to ask?"

Tom looked at his wife, turned around and went outside and paced as sprinkles of rain soaked his clothes. He muttered something Flora did not want to hear as he came back in the cabin.

All week, Flora worked on making flat circle bottoms and rows of coiled clay. She smoothed the sides with her paddle and a little water. Her bowls were plain and crude. Each one was better than the one before. She set them outside in the sun to dry. She didn't say a thing to Tom about them. He noticed but remained silent.

Every night Tom went to bed before Flora. She stayed up and worked on her baskets to pay her debt. She understood Tom's anger. They had lost their home from overspending. She felt this was different. She only owed $21.85, and when she finished four more baskets and sold another bunch of dried flowers, she'd give the money to pay her account at the hardware store and her debt would be paid.

Allen noticed the tense distance between his parents and went to his room every night to sketch after supper. He was almost glad when the rain stopped and his dad had to go back to the parkway construction site. He thought maybe a little distance and time would soothe the strained relationship with his parents. At least he hoped so.

Every day Flora piddled with the leather strap that allowed the peddle to lift up and down, but with no luck.

When she turned the wheel, it wobbled. Tom was still angry at her for purchasing it, so she didn't ask for his help when he came home on the weekend.

She asked her son. "Allen, I can't figure out how to keep the wheel from wobbling. Can you help me?" Allen looked at the torn strap. He spun the wheel and saw it wobbling. The bolt holding the strap was rusty. He got his dad's Three-in-One oil and soaked the bolt overnight. Flora left her son in the craft room sketching the potter's wheel. She busied herself in the kitchen.

Allen showed his sketch to Mr. Willard the next day and asked, "How do I fix it?"

Mr. Willard examined Allen's detailed drawing. He said, "The leather strap is easy. Measure the distance between the pedal and the base, then look at the width of the strap. You can cut a new leather strap and attach it. I think that will solve the problem."

"Where would I buy leather?" Allen asked.

"The hardware store should have it. He has everything," replied Mr. Willard

Still uncertain, Allen asked, "What about the wheel?"

Mr. Willard said, "Take it off. Have your dad or mom hold it straight as you refasten it."

Allen knew it would have to be his momma. His dad was still angry. Allen took the measurements to the hardware store. The owner wrote down the measurements, ambled to the back of the store, and cut the leather piece.

Allen asked how much he owed and handed the merchant a $20 bill. As the merchant made change, he said, "My mother had to charge part of the payment for the potter's wheel. How much does my momma owe?"

Allen took out three $10 bills and waited for the merchant to reply. He paid his mother's debt and asked for another block of clay. He brought the clay and leather strap into his mother's craft room and closed the door. The next afternoon, after school, he attached the leather strap as his momma held the wheel. It didn't wobble any more.

Tom was still angry. His anger shifted from Flora to Allen for fixing the wheel and buying his momma more clay. They had a heated argument about going against his father's wishes.

Allen turned toward his dad and in a loud voice said, "Your silent treatment hasn't solved anything. It is childish behavior. Momma has a right to try her hand as a potter. If she is good at it, she will make money, maybe more than she needed to pay off her charge. By the way, that bill has been paid. I paid it with some of the money I saved from working for Mr. McCord. She has a right to feel good about learning to weave and create pottery pieces." Allen turned and went to his room and slammed the door. Tom went out the front door and paced.

Flora stayed in the craft room and looked around. If she had known it was going to cause so many headaches, she wouldn't have bought the potter's wheel. She didn't know what to do.

She spoke out loud, "Have I made the wrong decision?"

She closed the door to the craft room and went into the kitchen. She wrung her hands and paced. She thought when Tom saw the wheel was fixed and she was making pieces, he'd calm down and be his mellow self again, but that wasn't happening.

At dusk, Tom came back inside and apologized to his wife and asked for her forgiveness. He explained it wasn't the wheel. It was the fact she owed money and she must have forgotten that was what caused them to lose the house, to yank their sons out of the only school and community they knew, and make such a strained adjustment for Allen. Tom knew his son was right. He had been acting childish.

He knocked on Allen's bedroom door. Allen yanked open the door and stood there with a look of disgust on his face.

His dad said, "Son, you were right. I was acting childish. I kept thinking it was indebtedness that caused us to lose everything. I thought the cycle of spending more than we could afford was starting again. I've apologized to your mother and I am apologizing to you for creating so much unhappiness. Thank you for helping your momma fix the potter's wheel. I didn't like your outburst, but I needed that to jar me back into reality."

A few days later, Emmy walked over to the Cole cabin. Flora showed her the wheel and Emmy removed the plastic from a block of clay and cut off a piece. She molded it into a ball and slammed it down and said, "This is called throwing clay. It takes the air bubbles out of the clay."

She put the piece on the wheel and began to peddle, using her hand to bore into the clay as it began to take shape.

Emmy stopped peddling and said, "Flora, you try it."

Flora's eyes got bigger and she smiled, then she began to laugh as the bowl took shape. It was crude, but it was a start.

Art Competition Surprises

In December 1947, Allen's drawings of the workers during the tobacco harvest were displayed near the office of the high school. Mr. Willard, the art teacher at the county high school, displayed students' projects in the school halls and selected the work of his most talented students for the county art exhibit and competition. Allen and Alecia's art projects were two of the pieces he planned to send to the county fair in April.

Allen kept a portfolio of all his drawings. He had a full artist pad of just birds. He had framed a few for his parents and one for Alecia as a Christmas present. He had another collection of mountain people, sunsets, and some of small creatures digging for food after the big snow. Art fascinated him.

On the last Saturday in April, Mr. and Mrs. Cole and Allen spent the day at the county fair. They watched children on rides and rode a few themselves. They visited the open tents with displays of canned vegetables, jellies, preserves and pickles. In the handcraft tent, Flora examined the needlework and patterns created. She kept looking for the tent with pottery and the grassy areas with wreaths and baskets. Allen and his dad wandered off to the wood craft displays.

Flora waved them off as she moved into the tent with all kinds of pottery. She picked up small round bowls and some tall ones that fanned out. She felt the texture of each piece and spoke to the potters. She was looking at the different variety of baskets when her husband and son found her and told her they were starved. Tom took her arm and headed to the food stands. Each had a cup of burgoo, cornbread, and a small bottle of soda pop before they searched for the art exhibit.

They entered the large wooden building to find adult art work on display in the first room. In the next room, elementary schoolchildren's work filled the walls from ceiling to floor. They entered the last room labeled "High School Works of Art". The room was filled with portable walls with various art mediums—pastels, acrylic, oil, watercolor and charcoal pictures and scenes.

They walked down the first two rows. Tom and Flora were impressed by the quality of the student art but saw none of their son's work. He had said some of his pieces were to be in the exhibit. As they started down the third row, Flora gasped, put one hand over her heart and grabbed her husband's arm with the other. Displayed at the end of the row on easels were the pictures of Flora and Alecia. Allen was equally surprised when he saw the two first place ribbons on his two entries.

Lonely Days and Nights

The semester ended and Peter wrote his parents that he'd take six semester hours in the summer session and continue his work for Mr. Cleburne on the farm.

He wrote, "If I go to summer school each year and take six hours, I will finish college in three years. I promise I will come home in late August before fall semester."

Flora was disappointed but understood. He was an adult and making his own decisions.

As promised, Michael McCord hired Allen for the summer. He joined his dad and the other men clearing the land for the mountain parkway. The distance from home was too great for them to come home every night. Camp sites were set up and the men went home on the weekends. Allen shared a tent with his dad. They were exhausted at the end of each day.

Tom and Allen were gone from Monday to Friday and sometimes on Saturday all summer, and now Peter wrote he wouldn't be home either.

The cabin was silent all the time. Flora decided to turn on the radio whenever she was inside. She'd listen to the news, sing along with the singers, and even listen to the baseball games as she embroidered pictures on their pillowcases or table scarves. She missed the shared meals each night and the swinging on the porch after supper. The music made the loneliness bearable.

She was accustomed to working her garden, tending the chickens and even using the push mower Tom had bought, so grass around the cabin was kept short. Daily, she weeded, gathered vegetables from the garden and canned. Some days she walked over to Emmy's just to have some human contact.

Flora had more time in the afternoon to gather grasses, vines and tender branches for basket weaving. She always had a bucket of thin branches soaking. While the grasses dried and the vines and small limbs soaked, she made simple pottery pieces. Each piece was of better quality than the one before. Her craft room shelves were filling up with an assortment of vases, bowls and unusual plates. She boiled berry juice to color the clay. She began to draw flowers and curls of vine on some.

To afford the clay and cheesecloth, she sold some of her smaller baskets to the mercantile store. She kept her larger ones in hopes of selling them at the October festival in Blyne.

Emmy came over many afternoons and used the potter's wheel. They hoped to have their own tent of wares to sell at the October festival in Blyne.

In September, they spent the day in flea markets and used goods stores in search of folding tables and chairs. The pickings were slim. At the end of the day, Emmy's car had two white sheets in need of bleaching, two folding tables in need of a lot of scrubbing, and several metal folding chairs. A coat of paint would make them look new. The only tents they saw were Army green tents from World War II, so they splurged and ordered one from the Sears & Roebuck catalog.

At the end of summer, Allen returned home to start his senior year of high school. He saved most of the money he'd earned to help pay for college, though he didn't know where he would go. His dad was still away during the week and would be for some time.

Flora asked Allen what kind of paint she should buy and what kinds of brushes to use to create designs and scenes on the pottery pieces. He recommended his mother should buy the set of brushes in a rolled canvas bag, and she did.

There were brushes with thin fibers to paint leaves and delicate shapes and thicker brushes to fill in larger objects. There were brushes with gaps between fibers to create bands of different colors. She had no idea how all of the brushes would be used but was fascinated at all the possibilities. Allen spent a few afternoons after school to teach his momma how and when to use each.

After the summer canning was complete, Flora and Emmy had more time to visit. Emmy came over often and used the potter's wheel. The two friends were creating something every day, so the shelves were quickly filled. They spent many afternoons in the craft room at the Coles' cabin while their husbands were on the parkway project.

At night they filled many lonely hours at home making baskets and wreaths.

They had taken pieces of pottery, wreaths and baskets to the Hopperville Art Center to sell, and some of their pieces sold before they could return with more. They were encouraged by visitors to the center who bought their creations. The two women were determined to have enough pieces to take to the Blyne October Festival at the end of the month.

Flora would be able to see her son, Peter, when they went to Blyne for the festival. Emmy was envious of her. She saw her son, Ted, on weekends. He worked alongside his stepfather, but it would be at least a year before she would see her older son, Jeb. He was in the Marines.

Emmy shared a letter from her son, Jeb. His unit had been assigned duty in North Carolina. He was learning to be an airplane mechanic. Emmy hadn't seen her son in over a year. She commented, "He loves the Marines and has talked of making it a career."

Flora told her Peter planned to finish college in three years and she didn't expect him to come home either.

Tom Cole and Michael McCord were too worn out after their week near the West Virginia line to go to Blyne, so Emmy and Flora packed Emmy's car and left the mountain at six o'clock that morning.

They could not figure out how to keep the tent from falling and decided to set up their tables and display their wares. They set the baskets too large for the tables on the grassy area beside them. The sales were good. They found the painted pottery brought a higher price, and the baskets were gone by mid-afternoon.

Peter and his girlfriend, Maria, stopped at their tables and helped them pack the car for home. It was dusk as they left Blyne. There was little traffic once they were away from the city. Emmy drove slower and was very quiet as she drove up the mountain and let Flora off. They had split the money they had earned and decided to unpack the car the next day when it was light and they weren't tired.

Tom greeted his wife with a kiss and asked if they had many sales. Flora opened her purse, pulled out the money, spread it like a fan in her hand and danced around, as Tom laughed.

The Brown Coupe

The mountain parkway construction meant Flora was alone at home most of the time. She'd have Tom's favorite foods cooked when he came home on Friday night and have his clothes washed and folded by Sunday evening for the next week's work.

Tom came home and longed for a good night's sleep in their bed and the company of his wife and son the rest of the weekend.

Flora felt Tom thought about his wants when he came home and never considered her need to do something or go somewhere outside of the cabin. Flora understood it was necessary for him to have those few hours to share with her and their son, Allen, but she felt trapped in the cabin.

Allen, a senior in high school, wanted to participate in the few functions the school had and he wanted as much time with Alecia as her parents would allow. Allen chopped and stacked wood for the house and shoveled the snow in winter, but he didn't have much time to spend with his momma, and she missed that quality time.

Yes, Tom and Allen had finished the addition of the craft room and the chicken space to the cabin. The chickens were safe. She could gather the eggs and droppings by going in the safe room. Her husband had given her a Singer sewing machine for Christmas, and her sons gave money for fabric. Yes, she had Emmy close by. Michael, Emmy's husband, was working with his construction crew. Emmy had lived in these mountains all her life and understood there would be separations. Emmy knew all the mountain people and had a car to visit or go places.

Flora didn't have people she visited. She had no means to go anywhere she needed for her craft supplies or food she wanted from the store. She had to ask her son or Emmy to take her. Flora had her crafts of weaving, quilting and pottery, but that did not make up for human contact. If she wanted to talk to her son in college, she had to go to the public phone in town. She never knew if he'd be at Yocum House.

Flora needed to find a way to have her independence from "cabin confinement." She thought about her isolation one day as Emmy drove her to the nearby town for cloth. She asked her, "Emmy, when did you learn to drive?"

Emmy had her eyes glued to the sharp curves of the road as she spoke. "When Daddy worked on stringing power lines and my granddaddy became too ill to plow the garden, he taught me. My granddaddy told me what to do. He didn't show me. He had me put a chair out by the garden where he sat. As I pointed to the different levers on the tractor, he told me their names and how and when to use them. You should have seen me try to back it up, turn it around, and give it either too much gas or not enough. I'd step on the gas instead of the clutch or brake. One day I made such a wide turn, granddaddy fell off his chair and rolled in the dirt to get away from me. That was the day he told me about using brakes again. It was stop and go of the worst kind. We had plenty of garden planted that year, but as a result of my driving, it looked like this zigzagged road we are traveling.

"When the war started and my daddy and my first husband, Luther, went to war, I drove my daddy's truck, though not very far. Gasoline was rationed. When I met and married Michael after my Luther was killed, he knew I could drive. I used Daddy's truck until Michael bought a truck. Sometimes he'd let me drive it, if I needed to go into town for something. He bought me this car three years ago. Why do you want to know about my driving?"

Flora didn't hesitate, "I want you to teach me how to drive. Anytime I want or need something, I have to ask you to drive me. Don't get me wrong. I like your driving but I impose on you too often.

"I've saved most of the money I have made from my quilts, pottery, baskets, and dried flower sales over the past two years. I have over $400. If sales are good at the county fair in two weeks, and the items I have on display at the Appalachian Art Center sell, I think I will have enough to buy a used car. I saw in the newspaper new cars cost between $1200-$1400. I think I could find a used one for about $500. Will you teach me how to drive?"

Emmy asked,"What does Tom think about you wanting to drive, and does he know you are planning to buy a car?"

Flora turned toward her friend with a big smile dancing across her face. She said, "I haven't told him yet and I'm not going to tell him. I'll show him after you teach me to drive and we go shopping for my car. Once I own it and show Tom I know how to drive, he'll have no say in the matter."

Emmy shook her head in disbelief. "Flora, you know what happened when you brought home the potter's wheel. He didn't speak to you for over a week. And when did I agree to go car shopping with you?"

Flora asked again, "Will you teach me to drive?"

"If I agree, where would you practice?"

Flora smiled. She knew Emmy was going to teach her and said, "We have four acres of land and half of it is cleared. I'll do like you did when you learned. You can tell me what you are doing and why as you circle my yard. Tell me when you change gears and why, and when you push down on the clutch and let off the gas—I think that is what I have seen you do—tell me why. Then we will change places and I'll be the driver. If I jerk the car at first, no one will know except you and me. If I back into a sapling, it will chip the tree but won't hurt this steel body.

My garden may look like a race track as I learn how to maneuver this big piece of steel."

Emmy rolled her eyes and shook her head in disbelief, but agreed to teach her.

*****.

When the two husbands left at sunrise on Monday morning, Flora scurried around the house doing her housework as Allen got ready for school. She was scooping up the chicken manure when he yelled goodbye. She heard the squeal of the tires as he left the yard. She bathed, dressed, and was sitting on the porch steps when Emmy pulled down the dirt drive to the Coles' cabin.

Every morning after Allen left for school, Emmy drove to the Coles' place. The first couple of days, Emmy did the driving and explaining. On Thursday of the first week, Flora did the driving while Emmy was the passenger. Emmy told Flora what to as her hands turned the steering wheel and her feet were moving on the floorboard in front of her.

Flora drove straight down the garden, turned around clusters of trees, and between trees, scraping a few. Flora had been driving for two weeks before Emmy's tense body relaxed, that is until Flora circled the cabin and drove out of the yard.

Emmy braced herself, thrust out her arms as if grabbing the steering wheel, and jammed her foot into the floorboard to apply the imaginary brake on the passenger side of the car. She asked in a voice of panic, "What are you doing?"

Flora didn't look at her friend. She said calmly, "I'm driving into town."

She drove onto the zigzagged road. She crept down the mountain and onto the main road toward town. There were few cars on the road at eleven o'clock in the morning. Emmy was relieved. She closed her eyes. She didn't want to see what Flora would do next. She felt Flora slow down, move to a curb, and stop the car. She opened her eyes to see Flora had parked in front of the used car lot. Flora got out of the car while Emmy got out with weak knees and followed her friend into the car lot.

Flora looked at each car and looked at each price painted on the windshield. The salesman came out and followed them around. He asked Flora what kind of car her husband wanted, whether he was looking for a specific model or did he have a certain amount to spend? Flora didn't respond. She looked at every car on the lot, waved to the flustered salesman and walked to the car.

Emmy reached for the keys Flora was holding and said, "I'll drive back up the mountain."

Flora closed her hand tightly around the keys and replied, "I drove down the mountain, so I'm going to drive back up the mountain."

Emmy stood there with her hand stretched out and her mouth open. She couldn't believe what she was hearing.

Flora climbed into the driver's seat, cranked the engine, and waited for Emmy to get in the car.

Emmy asked, "What was all that about?"

Flora said, "I was looking over the cars to see what 'll get for my money when I buy the brown coupe."

"What about a driver's license and insurance?" asked Emmy.

Flora smiled at Emmy and said, "After I pay for the car, I will drive to Hopperville and take the driver's test. It is only nine miles away."

Emmy was exasperated with her friend. Hadn't she learned anything about buying something without telling her husband? Now it was a car. Emmy didn't mention Flora's intentions to her husband, Michael, either. She was afraid he'd say something to Tom Cole.

*****

Flora and Emmy filled Emmy's car and Tom's truck with the tables and items they had made. There were quilts, pottery, baskets, dried flowers, jams and pickles for sale. That warm and sunny day had many customers with pockets full of money to spend.

They sold patterned red quilts for $40, vases and colorful bowls for $5 or $10, and decorated sets of dishes for $20. Bunches of dried flowers sold for $2, as did dried herbs in labeled bags. The wreaths Flora made sold for $7. They had all sizes of baskets on the grass. Very small ones sold for $3 and Flora's two wood and crochet three-goose baskets each sold for $25 after two ladies kept outbidding each other. Emmy took a sheet of paper and wrote down their total sales.

Tom and Michael were at the fair, but ventured off to see what the Amish men had made and to see if anyone was whittling. Tom had put a few sticks in his truck bed that morning, just in case. Occasionally, they went by their wives' tables. Michael asked if they had already sold all the pickles. Emmy realized the box with the pickles was still in the car. Michael brought them to their tables and helped set them out. He opened a jar, and he and Tom walked around munching them.

At dusk, the items not sold were put in Emmy's car, while the tables were placed in the bed of Tom's truck. They ate at the new cafeteria called Britter's; they had heard fair customers rave about the good food and desserts. The selection of food seemed endless. The pies piled high with meringue were too tempting to resist. Flora and Tom both commented how much they enjoyed the day. On the way home, Tom told Flora he was making enough money now that they could splurge once a month and eat out as they had done before their luck changed.

*****

Sunday afternoon, Flora walked through the path between the Cole and McCord property. Emmy and Flora counted the money they had made and divided it. They each made $167. Flora knew she had enough money to buy the brown coupe and a few dollars left over. She asked Emmy if she would take her into town on Tuesday to buy the car, then go to Hopperville to get her license. Emmy hesitantly agreed to take her. Flora tucked the money in her dress pocket and walked back to the cabin.

A redbud tree was in full bloom beside the path and she picked a limb of redbud flowers for the vase on the kitchen table. She smiled as she came into the clearing by the cabin and saw Tom swinging.

Her husband's feet were pushing the porch swing back and forth and watching for her to return. She sat down beside him. He noticed the redbuds in her hand and pulled the branch up to his nose to inhale the fragrance. She smiled. He winked at her as he continued to push the swing. She didn't volunteer to tell him how much money she had made at the fair, so he asked. Flora told him her portion was $167.

He whistled, then said, "Maybe before next year's fair, I can make walking sticks to sell."

He asked her, "What are you going to do with the money?"

She replied, "I've got a project in mind. If I can do it, you will be proud of me."

*****

Tom left Monday morning for the construction site, wondering if new furniture or one of those new washing machines might be her project. No need guessing. He'd know soon enough.

She'd Earned Enough

Monday, after her chores, Flora took the cloth bag she had stuffed out of the mattress and counted the money she had made over the past two years from sales of her wares at the Blyne October festival, the Appalachian Art Center, and last year's county fair. She had $567.

Tuesday morning, Flora haggled with the car salesman for over an hour and got the car for $475.00. Gas sold for nineteen cents a gallon, so she asked for two dollars' worth. The attendant pumped the gas, cleaned the windshield, checked the tires, oil, and water level. Emmy followed her out of the gas station and drove behind her the nine miles to Hopperville.

Flora had a smile on her face as she waved to her friend and opened the door to the transportation center. She took the written test and came back outside with the officer holding a clipboard. He checked everything on the car to make sure they worked. The officer got in the car with Flora and fifteen minutes later the brown coupe pulled up to the door. She and the officer went inside the transportation building. A few minutes later, Flora came out of the center waving her driver's license. In celebration, Flora took her friend to lunch before driving back home.

*****

Allen came home at dusk and noticed the car parked in the yard. He wondered who was visiting. He looked around when he came into the cabin but only saw his mother. He asked, "Whose car is in the yard?"

Flora didn't turn around from the stove as she commented, "It's mine. I bought it today then drove to Hopperville to get my license."

Allen shouted, "WHAT? DOES DAD KNOW ABOUT THIS? When did you learn how to drive? Momma, you know how angry Dad got when you brought home the potter's wheel. He is going to be furious. You have got to tell him I had nothing to do with this."

She put the food on the table and said, "We will discuss this on Friday when your dad gets home."

She reached for his hand and said the blessing. All week she practiced her speech to her husband about the car. She told herself she'd be calm as she had been with Allen, at least that was what she hoped.

Tom came home Friday afternoon, kissed his wife, and asked, "Allen got one of his buddies over? He's got a nice looking car. Who is it?"

Flora held onto the large wooden spoon she had in her hand, as she answered in a soft, calm voice, "No, he doesn't have a friend visiting. That's my car. I bought it with the money I've earned over the past two years."

Tom yelled, "WHAT DID YOU SAY?"

She put the wooden spoon down, put her hands on her hips, and said, "It's mine. You leave every Monday morning and don't get back until Friday. When you come home, you're exhausted. I am alone in this cabin all week. If I need or want something in town or if I want to take crafts to the art center, I have to ask Emmy to drive me. No more. I have my own wheels.

"If Allen's art teacher is right, he will get a scholarship to that art school in Atlanta, and if your job continues to take you away all week, I'll be more alone. I bought it. It is paid. There is no debt, if that is why you are angry."

Red-faced and in an angry voice, Tom growled, "It is not a woman's place to go off and buy a car, when you know nothing about cars. You driving is not reasonable. Have you forgotten there are bootleggers all over this mountain? It is not safe for you to drive. The mountain road twists, and is full of potholes. You could have an accident. Can't you remember how bad the road is when it is icy or has heavy snow covering it? NO, FLORA, YOU CAN'T KEEP THAT DAMN CAR! By the way, who taught you to drive?"

Flora said nothing. She listened to his argument, but knew she owned that car, and she was going to drive it no matter what he said.

Tom walked back and forth, shaking his head, turned and looked at her, and went outside, slamming the door. A few minutes later, Tom came in and started to say something.

Flora turned her back to him and said, "It's my car. I paid for it. I'm keeping it. I am driving it to Blyne to see Peter on Sunday. You can ride with me, drive yourself, or stay home."

Tom did not move. His wife picked up a dish and the ladle to put the stew on the plates for dinner. They ate in silence. The silence continued until breakfast the next morning.

Tom got up first and made the coffee. Poured himself a cup and went outside. He walked to the brown coupe and checked the tires, looked for dents and rust spots. He raised the hood and checked the hoses, checked the oil and water levels. He closed the hood and got in the car. He checked the lights, stepped on the brake pedal, the clutch and gas pedal. The key was in the ignition and he started the motor. It had a smooth humming sound. He turned the car off.

Flora had smelled the coffee brewing and got up. From the bedroom window she had watched him check out the car. She dressed and went in the kitchen to start breakfast.

Tom came in the cabin but made no mention of examining the car. He wasn't aware she had watched him examine the car from the window. She was making the pancakes and frying the bacon when he came inside and poured himself a second cup of coffee, then sat at the kitchen table.

He turned toward her and in a calm voice said, "I looked over your car. Everything works and appears to be in good condition."

After breakfast, he walked to the McCords' house and spoke with Michael McCord. McCord came outside. Tom greeted him and spoke about how nice it felt with a crisp breeze. McCord nodded. Tom stood there for a minute, then commented, "I guess you know Flora bought a car. We had some very heated words about her buying a car without telling me."

McCord nodded his head and said, "Emmy told me last night about the car. Tom, Emmy taught her how to drive and said she is a careful driver. You and I are gone all week. Flora can now go into town or visit the ladies from church. She won't be trapped in that cabin. It means she'll be a happier wife when you get home on Friday afternoon. Go home and apologize to Flora for your temper. Let her drive to church tomorrow. It is only two miles from your cabin."

Tom remarked, "I can't believe she did this without talking to me first. Maybe she realized how I'd react. Thanks, Michael, for the advice. I need to go and try to apologize to my wife. I just can't believe she did this behind my back."

Flora was hanging his clean clothes on the clothesline when he stopped at the end of the path to their cabin. Tom thought about the argument the night before. His wife was wrong. She should have talked to him before she did such a foolish thing as buying a car when she knew nothing about cars. He could feel the anger inside him. He shook his head and muttered, "I can't forgive her."

Tom kept hearing McCord's comment in his head all afternoon as he sat in his chair.

Neither spoke until supper and they held hands for the blessing. Both were hurting, but both were too stubborn to make peace. At bedtime, Tom turned toward the window to sleep and Flora turned toward the bedroom wall.

Flora Is the Driver

Flora got up early and fixed breakfast. Tom and Allen smelled the ham and eggs and appeared at the breakfast table as she placed the hot food on their plates. She filled the three coffee cups, then sat down and put her hands out to her two hungry men for the blessing.

Tom felt the warmth of his wife's hand and tightened his hold even after the blessing was said. He was still wrestling with how to accept that she had bought a car. He struggled with how to apologize for his anger Friday evening when she told him she bought the brown coupe.

Allen looked around the kitchen for the basket of food they usually took with them when they visited his brother, Peter. He asked, "Are we still going to Blyne after church?"

Flora replied, "Yes, I decided I'd take our family to lunch at the big restaurant in town. I sent Peter a postcard on Wednesday and asked him to meet us there."

She cleared the table, then went in the bedroom to dress for church. She picked up her purse and walked to her car and got in. Allen climbed in the back seat. Tom opened the passenger door and sat beside his wife.

Flora turned toward her husband and said, "Tom, I know how to drive. Don't be so gloomy."

Slowly, Flora pulled out of the yard and onto the road. Allen moved to the edge of the backseat and put his head between his parents so he could watch his momma drive. She said nothing. She had to prove to both her husband and son that she knew how to drive.

As she approached a pothole, both Tom and Allen got tense. She went around it and both relaxed. Flora smiled and continued toward church. Neither questioned her driving the rest of the way to the church. She parked the car away from the few automobiles and trucks at church. Tom took Flora's hand as they walked to the church door and went inside.

The sermon that morning was about forgiveness. Normally, Tom heard the minister's words, but didn't feel they applied to him. Today was different. He needed to apologize to Flora for his temper outburst. He needed her forgiveness.

Flora thought about the message of the minister's sermon, and knew she needed to ease the tension between them. He'd made one concession. He'd ridden with her and didn't criticize her driving. As they walked to the car after church, he took his wife's hand and asked her to forgive him for his anger.

She replied with a nod of yes and said, "I was wrong in not telling you first. Forgive me."

Tom opened the car door for his wife, then still holding her hand, he asked, "Do you want me to drive to Blyne since it's so far away and you haven't driven on a highway very much?"

Flora didn't respond. She got in the driver's seat as she released her hand from his. Tom walked to the passenger's side and got in the car. Tom and Allen watched every move Flora made for the first few miles, then turned their attention to the scenery on the side of the road.

Peter was standing in front of the restaurant when his mother parked the car. He whistled as he came over to the car and looked it over. His mother got out of the car, smiled and gave her son a hug.

They seated themselves in the restaurant near the big picture window and looked over the menu. A young girl put down three glasses of water and then took out a notepad to take the orders. All four ordered the country fried steak dinner and a bowl of apple cobbler with ice cream for dessert.

As they ate, Flora told her family of how she watched Emmy drive and followed her instructions as she went up and down the yard. They laughed as she told of the crooked rows she'd created when she first attempted to drive.

They walked the town square as a family. Flora looked at every shop's displays. She made a mental note of what crafts she saw and the asking prices. Jokingly, Peter asked her what she was going to do next with the money she was going to earn with the sale of her crafts. Without hesitation she said, "I'm going to buy a Bendix Deluxe washing machine that will do the washing for me." Another round of laughter as they walked to the car.

Flora reached inside the back seat of the car and handed Peter his tin of cookies. He gave his mother a hug. She turned to her husband and offered the car keys and asked if he wanted to drive home.

Recipes

Corn Bread

1 egg, beaten

1 Tbsp. baking powder

1 1/2 cups buttermilk

1/2 tsp. baking soda

1/4 cup canola or vegetable oil

1 Tbsp. sugar

1 ½ cups corn meal

1 cup all-purpose plain flour

Directions:

Sift together all dry ingredients. In a mixing bowl add egg, buttermilk and oil. Mix until smooth. Slowly add dry ingredients, mixing between each addition. Put into a greased deep-dish pie plate or 9-inch cake pan. Bake at 400 degrees for 20-25 minutes. It is done when it springs back when touched.

(Alternative cooking method. Spoon batter onto a hot oiled griddle as you would for pancakes. As with pancakes, flip the corn cakes over when batter bubbles. Flat corn cakes are ready in just a few minutes.)

White Bread

1 pkg. dry yeast

4-5 cups all-purpose flour

1/4 cup warm water (105-115 degrees)

2 Tbsp. sugar

1 1/3 cups warm water

2 Tbsp. Crisco

Extra Crisco to grease pans

Directions:

Sift 4 cups of flour, salt and sugar in a large mixing bowl. Add Crisco and work into flour mix. Dissolve yeast in ¼ cup of warm water. Add to flour mix. Add water a little at a time until it is soft and elastic enough that it barely sticks to your fingers and pulls away from the sides of the bowl. Pull dough to one side and grease with a little Crisco, then do the other side. Cover the bowl with a towel and place it in a warm place until bread doubles in size, about an hour. Grease 2 (8 or 9 inch) baking pans with a little Crisco. Knead dough on a floured surface until smooth. Divide dough in half. Roll dough to fit pan. Place seam-side down. Cover and place in a warm spot until dough doubles in size, about an hour. Bake at 400 degrees for 33 minutes. Makes two loaves.

Blackberry Cobbler

6 cups blackberries

2 Tbsp. corn starch

1/4 cup melted butter

2 1/2 cups all-purpose flour

1 1/2 cups sugar

1 tsp. salt

2 cups milk

1 Tbsp. vanilla

Directions

Preheat oven to 350 degrees.

Lightly grease a 9x13 baking dish with butter. In a large bowl pour the blackberries. Add the cornstarch and ½ cup of sugar. Drizzle ¼ cup of melted butter over berries. Toss berries until all are coated. Spread berry mix in baking dish. In another bowl place flour, sugar, salt and baking powder. Mix. Add milk to dry ingredients and add vanilla. Mix. Pour over berries and bake for 1 hour.

Snow Ice Cream

1/3 cup of sugar

1 can condensed milk

2 eggs

3 cups sweet milk

1 tsp. vanilla

Snow

Directions

Mix all ingredients except snow. Add snow to thicken the ice cream.

Old Fashioned Sugar Cookies

1/2 cup butter flavored Crisco

1/2 cup sugar

1 egg, beaten

1 tsp. vanilla

1/2 cup sour cream

2 1/2 cups all-purpose flour

1 tsp. baking powder

3/4 tsp. salt

1/2 tsp. baking soda

Sugar to sprinkle on cookies

Directions

Cream Crisco and sugar. Add egg and vanilla. Add sour cream. Mix. Sift dry ingredients. Slowly add to liquids and beat until all is mixed. Chill dough thoroughly. Roll out to ½ - 1 inch thick. Cut with a cookie cutter. Sprinkle lightly with sugar and press into the cookies. Bake at 350 degrees for 15 minutes. Makes 4 dozen cookies.

Gingerbread Cookies

3 cups all-purpose flour

1 egg

1 tsp. baking soda

1 stick unsalted butter

3/4 tsp. cinnamon

1/4 cup butter-flavored Crisco

3/4 tsp. ground ginger

1/2 cup dark brown sugar, packed

1/2 tsp. allspice

2/3 cup unsulfured molasses

1 tsp. nutmeg

1/2 tsp. cloves

½ tsp. salt

Directions

Sift all dry ingredients together. In a large bowl, cream butter, Crisco and brown sugar. Add egg and mix. Add molasses and mix thoroughly. Slowly add dry ingredients. Mix after each addition. Divide dough into two parts. Form into balls and wrap with plastic wrap. Refrigerate for 3-4 hours. Take one dough ball from the refrigerator at a time. Unwrap the ball and let it sit a few minutes to soften enough to roll out on a lightly floured surface (I use waxed paper).

Roll dough to ¼ inch thickness. Cut with a cookie cutter that has been dipped in flour. Bake at 375 degrees for 10-12 minutes until edges begin to brown. Cool on the baking sheet for 10 minutes before removing. Repeat the process with the second ball of dough. Use a fresh sheet of waxed paper that has been floured. Use store bought tube icing to decorate. Makes 3 dozen

*** **This is a soft cookie. For a harder cookie roll dough to 1/8 inch.**

Pound Cake

1 lb. (2 cups) butter

2 1/2 cups sifted cake or all-purpose flour

10 eggs, separated

2 cups sugar

1 tsp. vanilla

10 egg whites

Directions

Cream butter. Add flour and work in until mealy. Beat egg yolks, sugar and vanilla until fluffy. Add the flour/butter mixture to egg mixture. Beat until thoroughly mixed. In a separate bowl, beat the egg whites until stiff. Fold egg whites into batter (do not use a mixer.) Pour into greased bundt cake pan or 2 loaf pans. Bake for 75 minutes at 325 degrees. Cool in pan for 10 minutes before removing.

Chocolate Pound Cake

2 sticks margarine

1/2 cup cocoa

1/2 cup butter flavored Crisco

5 eggs

3 cups sugar

1 tsp. vanilla

3 cups sifted plain flour

1 cup milk

1/2 tsp. baking powder

Pinch of salt

Directions

Cream margarine and Crisco. Sift dry ingredients. Add to the creamed mixture. Add eggs one at a time. Blend well. Add vanilla. Grease and lightly flour a bundt pan or two loaf pans. Pour batter into pan and bake at 350 degrees for 1 ½ hours. DO NOT OPEN THE OVEN DOOR WHILE BAKING. Frost the cake with Cocoa Coffee Icing.

Cocoa Coffee Icing

1 1/2 Tbsp. butter

2 cups powdered sugar

2 1/2 Tbsp. cocoa

Strong black coffee

Beat butter and cocoa together until blended. Sift and beat sugar into mix. Add enough black coffee for a smooth consistency.

Vegetable Soup

1 lb. (93/7) ground beef

64 oz. bottle V-8

1 medium onion, chopped

3-4 stalks celery, sliced 1-inch thick

2 large potatoes, peeled and cut

1 can English peas and juice

1 can cut green bean and juice

3 carrots, sliced

1 Tbsp. dried parsley

Salt and pepper to your taste

64 oz. water

Directions

Brown ground beef so there is no pink. If 93/7 lean beef is used, there is no grease. If you use beef with more fat, drain it off. In an 8-quart soup pot, pour in the V-8 juice. Rinse bottle with water and add to the pot. Add meat and all vegetables. Let it come to a boil, then turn down to medium. Cook for approximately an hour.

*** **Optional: Add a cup of uncooked elbow macaroni to soup the last 15 minutes.**

Fried Rabbit

I have never cooked rabbit. My mother fried rabbit when I was a child and made a rich brown gravy. My father was a merchant. He sold rabbit purchased from a meat packing company. This recipe is from the cookbook my mother used, *Culinary Arts Institute Encyclopedia Cookbook,* edited by Ruth Berolzheimer. My mother gave me a copy when I got married in 1961.

2 young rabbits (2 ½ to 3 pounds)

2 egg yolks, beaten

3 cups milk

1 1/4   cups all-purpose flour

1 tsp. salt

 1/2 cup fat

2 tsp. currant jelly

1 Tbsp. minced parsley

Directions

Wash dressed rabbit thoroughly under running water. Dry. Cut into serving pieces. Combine egg and 1 cup of milk and slowly add 1 cup of flour and salt. Beat until smooth. Dip rabbit in batter and fry in fat for about 15 minutes until brown. Reduce heat and continue cooking 30-40 minutes until tender. Stir frequently.

To make gravy, add remaining flour to pan with fat. Stir constantly Gradually add the remaining milk, salt and pepper to taste. Bring to a boil, stirring constantly until thickened. Pour over rabbit with jelly and parsley. Serves 6-8.

Yeast Rolls

1   pkg. dry yeast

1/2   cup warm water (105-115 degrees)

1 Tbsp. shortening

 2 Tbsp. sugar

2 tsp. salt

1/2 cup milk, scalded

2 eggs, beaten

3 1/2 to 4 cups all-purpose flour, sifted

Directions:

Soften yeast in ½ cup of water. Add shortening, sugar and salt to the scalded milk. Cool to lukewarm and add yeast and beaten egg. Sift in flour to make a soft dough. Place on a floured board and knead until dough is satiny and smooth. Let stand 10 minutes. Put in a greased bowl and cover; let rise until double in size. Punch down and let stand for 10 minutes. Shape into rolls and let stand to double in size. Bake at 425 degrees for 12 to 15 minutes.   Makes 24 rolls.

Pancakes

1 1/2 cups all-purpose flour

2 egg yolks, beaten

Tbsp. sugar

1 1/3 cup milk

1/2 tsp. baking powder

2 TBSP. butter, melted

1/4 tsp. salt

2 egg whites

Directions

Combine the flour, sugar, baking powder and salt in a bowl. Add mixture of egg yolks and milk. Beat until blended and smooth. Beat in the melted butter. Beat egg whites until stiff. Spread over batter and fold together. Lightly grease a preheated griddle (or skillet). Pour batter onto griddle from a pitcher or end of a large spoon. Turn pancakes when they are puffy and full of bubbles.

About the Author

Josephine Graven, known to most as Jo, is the mother of four children, grandmother of six adult grandchildren, and one great-grandson.

Mrs. Graven attended Jacksonville State College in Alabama and is a three- time graduate from the University of Alabama in Birmingham with reading endorsements at the masters and advance certification(a second master's degree) in education. Her twenty-nine years of classroom teaching were in Catholic school, public school and military dependent schools. Jo served two additional years as administrative intern for the assistant superintendent of curriculum at Fort Knox Military Dependent Schools. She was a Kentucky trained mentor teacher for first year teachers.

Jo was twice recognized as Elementary Teacher of the Year for the Tarrant City School System in Alabama and represented the school district for Jacksonville State University Teacher Hall of Fame. She is listed in Who's Who Among American Educators and Who's Who Among American Teachers. Ms. Graven has been a member of Delta Kappa Gamma International Society for 25 years and has served as president of a local chapter in Kentucky and twice in Alabama. She is a past president of the Lincoln Heritage Reading Council in Kentucky.

Mrs. Graven was a co-recipient of a Kentucky Center for the Arts Grant. Jo has given workshops in educational curriculum and storytelling at the local, district, state and southeastern conferences.

Ms. Graven has written for her alumni quarterly news booklet for over ten years. She has authored two seasonal cookbooks and co-authored a third cookbook. Jo is a storyteller who writes most of her material. She was a member of Tale Talk and E.A.R.S. storytelling groups in Kentucky. Jo is a member of Story Jammers storytelling group in Baldwin County, Alabama. She was one of four Gulf Coast storytellers featured in the Mobile Bay Magazine in 2012.